THE MERRY MÉNAGE

THE MERRY MÉNAGE

ANONYMOUS

Carroll & Graf Publishers, Inc.
New York

First Carroll & Graf edition 1992

Carroll & Graf Publishers, Inc.
260 Fifth Avenue
New York, NY 10001

ISBN: 0-88184-831-X

Manufactured in the United States of America

THE MERRY MÉNAGE

INTRODUCTION

It is hardly surprising when one looks into Victorian morality, that appearances were to be held high in importance, and behaviour, only secondary, if misbehaviour were discreetly indulged in. Such is the code of morality in "THE MERRY MENAGE," a manuscript that clearly mirrors the social and sexual behaviour of ladies and gentlemen of fashion.

Two widows and a virginal companion cheerfully invite the stud services of the guardian and mentor, and all is acceptable, including a menáge a quatre, provided there is no scandal.

The characters in this novel are based on actual persons in actual situations. The family, itself, was

11

highly respected and at no time did a breath of scandal so much as tarnish one initial of the good name of these 'good' people.

Documents, if reliable, would have it that the widow Helen, eventually marries Jack and the rich, young widowed daughter, Maud lives in the same household, thereby implementing now a menage á trois. There is no further reference to the young Alice, who served as a companion earlier. It is hoped that she was suitably rewarded, and what is more, respectably placed in appreciation of her services rendered.

The novelette "Old Fashioned Discipline," included as an addendum, was originally in the hands of collectors and has just recently become available for publication.

Editor

BOOK I

CHAPTER ONE

One morning, when I came down to breakfast, ι found the following letter of my plate:

The Nunnery, Wednesday.

Dear Jack,

What are you doing with yourself? I have come here ιor a ιew days, but find the place most terribly duιl, only Mother anα Alice being here. Can't you come down for a long week enα and αmuse three lonely females: ι am writing at Mother's suggestion. Do come!

Yours ever.

The invitation was very welcome. I *was* at a loose end, that week, and London in July is not the pleasantest of places. The Nunnery was a charming house to visit, so promptly I wired grateful acceptance, adding that I would arrive that same afternoon by tea time.

Now allow me to introduce my reader to my Dramatis Personae and to the scene.

"Mother" was my old friend, Mrs. Helen Bell; we were children together, and I was present at her wedding and godfather to her only child, Maud, my correspondent. Helen was scarcely seventeen when she married. Maud was born the following year, and was now twenty-two; Mrs. Bell was therefore not yet forty, and was frequently taken for Maud's elder sister. She now was in her prime, a splendidly shaped woman, rather tall, slightly inclining towards embonpoint but very graceful in her movements, and very attractive. Her husband had died three years ago, and had left her a pretty place and ample means; and her re-marriage had been confidently predicted but so far she had shewn no desire to re-enter into the wedded state.

She lived quietly and was the Lady Bountiful of the neighbourhood. She was wonderfully free of prejudices and particularly tolerant of the frailties of her own sex.

Maud, her daughter, was also a widow, her husband having died just a year ago, leaving her well provided for so long as she did not marry again, and lived "a chaste and proper life," to quote from his will. I was her Trustee as well as her godfather, and it devolved on me to see that the conditions of the will were conformed to. But she was of a particularly ardent temperament—as also was her mother—and her involuntary cry of dismay when she heard her husband's will read warned me that there would be trouble unless I took care.

She was a beautiful girl, having inherited her mother's good looks together with her father's height,—in fact she was unusually tall. She possessed a most voluptuous figure and loved to display it. Unlike her mother (who was a brunette) Maud was a charming blonde with a mass of golden hair and blue eyes, which fairly captivated me when after some years absence from England I returned home just in time for her wedding and I found myself horribly envious of the good fellow whom she married and who thus obtained the fullest rights over her charms! On his death my duties as her Trustee constantly brought us into close relations, and it was impossible for me not to note how her enforced celibacy was distressing her, while she could not but be aware of my passion for her. One day when I was nearly mad with desire after her and she had been unusually confidential, I ventured to suggest that so long as the Trustee was satisfied in his capacity as such, he in his capacity as godfather and dear friend might afford her the relief she so ardently craved. She delightedly conferred on me the further appointment of lover, and as opportunities presented themselves she received in my arms the solace that her ardent feminine temperament required from time to time, the happy gratification of which tended to heighten and ripen her attractions as well as to maintain her in perfect health.

"Alice" was Mrs. Bell's companion, practically her adopted daughter. Her mother was a school-mate and dear friend of Mrs. Bell; and on her death the latter took charge of Alice (who was totally unprovided for) and had her educated prop-erly. When Maud married, Mrs. Bell brought Alice home as her companion. She was a charming little maiden of that almost indescribable English type that necessitates the use of adjectives such as "sweet," "cuddlesome," "dainty," "scrumptious," etc., a universal favorite and one of the accepted belles of the neighbourhood; and although she had only just turned eighteen she had received more than one good offer of marriage, all of which she had refused. Mrs. Bell used to say half in fun and half in earnest that Alice was in love with me and that no one else would ever get her. I cannot say that I reciprocated the affection, but I will confess that I began to think Alice was a flower the pluck-ing of which would be a treat for a god.

She absolutely worshipped Mrs. Bell, and what-ever her own private opinions and ideas might be she was ready to conform to the slightest wish Mrs.

Bell might express—a characteristic that will be found to greatly affect the events that I am about to relate.

Mrs. Bell's residence, *"The Nunnery,"* was a comfortable old-fashioned house that stood in its own grounds some four miles from a country town. There were really two buildings, the house itself, and the wing that contained the domestic offices and the servants' rooms. The house had a ground floor and first floor; a sort of one storeyed passage gave the servants access—so that at night the family and visitors were quite separated from the domestics, a feature that also will be found to affect my narrative. Mrs. Bell's bedroom occupied the whole of one end, and looked out over the grounds, and communicated with Alice's bedroom and the room generally allotted to visitors by curtained doors.

As I journeyed down I wondered whether Maud's invitation meant anything of special significance. I knew that she had told her mother of our relations, and that Mrs. bell in her broad-minded way did not object (in view of the terms of the will and knowing her daughter's erotic temperament) so long as no scandal arose. But to allow Maud and me to have each other under her own roof seemed to me too improbable to be expected.

Maud met me at the station. She was driving herself in a waggonette without a groom. My light

19

baggage was soon put inside—I took my place beside her and we started off for *"The Nunnery"*.

When clear of the town the road began a long and somewhat steep ascent. Maud made the horse walk, then turning to me said: "Now Jack, I want to talk to you seriously."

"Good Heaven!, what have I done now!" I exclaimed.

Maud laughed. "It is not what you have done but what you are required to do that I want to talk about!" she replied; "now Jack, be a good boy and promise you'll do as we all want—all of us mind!"

"Of course I will if I can!", I rejoined gallantly —"what is it?—anything very serious or very difficult?"

Maud shook with laughter. "Jack, you're too funny! Yes!, it is very serious and it may be difficult! I'm going to call a spade a spade as it will be the easiest and quickest way! Jack, we all—all, mind you, including Alice—want you to ... have us! There!"

"What!", I exclaimed, staring at her in absolute surprise.

"It's quite true, Jack dear!" Maud replied, colouring faintly, "that's what we want you to do! Now listen!"

"I've been wanting you badly, my lover!—oh so badly—till I told mother that either you must come to me or I must go to you! She didn't like your having me under her own roof! I didn't want to go up to Town! A sudden idea struck me! As you know, Jack, Mother is still a young woman,—I get my hot temperament from her, and I know how she hates her lonely bed! And she loves you, Jack! So I slipped my arm round her, and whispered coaxingly: Look here, Mummy, let us get Jack down and . . . share him! She blushed like a schoolgirl! "Mummy," I again whispered—" you know you want . . . something . . . very badly, just as badly as I do!— (she quivered responsively)— won't you let me get it for you?—(again she blushed deeply). — "Come, Mummy darling, share Jack with me!" And I kissed her and kept whispering—it's sweet of you! if Jack is willing it shall be as you wish!" "There, Sir, what do you say?"

"I'm lost in astonishment!" I stammered—and so I was! "Maud," I added presently, "you're not playing a trick on me, are you?"

"I'm telling you God's truth, Jack!" she replied speaking now quite seriously and looking me straight in the eyes. "You won't say "No" to Mother, will you Jack?".

"Of course not, dear!" I replied as I placed my hand on hers—I place myself absolutely at your disposal and hers in all honour and loyalty, and will not spare myself in your service!"

Maud looked lovingly at me and I saw her eyes were dewy. Presently she said softly "Thank you for what you have said, my own true lover. I am proud and happy to think that you will at my request do to Mother what you have so often done so sweetly to me!" Then after a pause she added in a lighter vein "And you'll find your virtue being its own reward, Jack!—for Mother is a lovely woman, Sir!"

I laughed. "But what about little Alice!", I asked.

"Oh! we managed to square her without much difficulty!", Maud replied, smiling at the recollection." You know Jack, that Alice will do anything if Mother wishes her to do it. We got her quietly the same afternoon, and told her that we both were getting very anxious about her because we could see that her stifled natural desires were beginning to affect her health and looks! She was awfully staggered! Then Mother drew her on her lap and took her in her arms, kissed her tenderly and said lovingly: "My darling, my second daughter, the one man in the world we believe your love is coming down here for a few days, your Jack! (Alice blushed deeply)—if you will consent to let him put you right, Maud and I will keep you company and let him have us also, so that we can be together in my room where we can look after you! Will you consent, darling?" Poor Alice didn't know what to say—she was dreadfully taken aback! "Say yes, darling?" whispered Mother lovingly. Slowly came the answer "If you wish it, Auntie, Yes!" Between us we hugged and kissed and soothed her, and now she's all right about it though very timid! Jack, you're going to be a lucky man!"

"Going to be!" I exclaimed, looking tenderly at her as my hand slid on to her leg and amorously pressed the region of Love—"am I not so already, seeing that I have the run of this treasure!"—and again my hand rested over the organ of her sex! "And as if that was not enough luck for any man, you are going to put me in possession of the finest woman and the prettiest girl in this part of the County! Maud darling, how can I ever thank you sufficiently?"

Maud laughed wickedly. "Just keep a little bit in hand for me, darling," she replied,— "we are going to work you very hard, but don't forget my brokerage!"

I laughed. "If there should be only one drop left in me and you want it, darling, you shall have it! Now tell me, how do you propose to work this job? —have you made out a list of hours and appointments for me as they do for stallions, or am I to sit on the landing till some door opens and I am beckoned in?"

Maud laughed amusedly. "You must arrange all that with Mother after tea," she said— "she wants a talk with you and I have arranged to take Alice off, so as to leave you together. *Entre nous*, Jack, I think her idea is that we shall always meet in her bedroom as soon as the house is quiet, attired only in our "nighties", and there and then decide on the

23

evening's programme." As she spoke we drove through the gates. "There she is! . . . see, she has got Alice by the hand so as to make her meet you and get it over! . . . how Alice is blushing!"

"We're delighted to see you, Jack dear!" said Mrs. Bell as we alighted. "We were so glad to get your wire saying you would come!" And she kissed me affectionately, somewhat to Maud's surprise, for this was an unusual proceeding.

"You don't know how glad I was to get out of town, Helen!", I replied as I returned her salute. "How are you, Alice?—why, you're not looking quite yourself!" I added as I took her little hands in mind and drew her towards me— "I really must look after you!", I continued, as for the first time I kissed her virgin cheeks, now covered with blushes at what she evidently thought was a reference to the trouble alleged by Mrs. Bell and Maud. They regarded her affectionately, but I could see they had difficulty to smother a smile at my audacity and its effect on Alice.

"Show Jack his room, Maud", said Mrs. Bell as she passed her arm lovingly round the still blushing Alice— "tea will be ready in five minutes, and I expect you will want it!"

"Jack! how could you!" exclaimed Maud, choking with laughter when we reached the security of my room— "poor Alice! how a certain part of her must have tingled!"

"I couldn't help it!" I replied, as I joined in her

24

silent mirth "it was a sudden inspiration, and I think a happy one!"

"Very!", she rejoined—then pressed herself amorously against me looking tenderly into my eyes. I divined her desire and whispered softly "Finger or tongue, darling?"

"Finger!" she murmured—" no time for the other just now, but I must have something quickly!" Promptly I dropped into an easy chair and took her on my knees—as my hand stole up under her clothes and travelled along her delicious legs she threw her arms round my neck, pressed her lips on mind, and parted her thighs to assist my hand which just then was searching for the slit in her drawers—which it soon found; then my eager fingers rested on the already moist lips of Maud's cunt, now throbbing and pouting with sexual excitement! Hugging me tightly to her, Maud now began to wriggle on my knees in the most divine way as she felt my finger penetrate her cunt in delicious agitation and then craftily attack her excited clitoris! "Oh! Jack! ... oh! ... d-a-r-l-i-n-g!!," she gasped brokenly in blissful ecstasy!—then straining me to her she ejaculated "I'm coming!! ... I'm coming !!! ... oh! finish me!!" Promptly my finger played on her clitoris!—I felt an indescribable quiver pass through her—and then she inundated my happy finger with a profuse emission as her head dropped on my shoulder in her ecstatic rapture!

I allowed her to rest undisturbed by any movement on my part till she recovered from her half-swoon. As she came to herself, Maud drew a long breath, slowly raised her head—then looking lovingly at me with still humid eyes she passionately kissed me, murmuring. "Oh! darling! that was good!", and slowly rose from off my knees. Suddenly she stooped and whispered in my ear "Shall I do anything to you, Jack?" at the same time placing her hand gently on the fly of my trousers. I shivered with delight at her touch and nearly yielded to temptation, but retained sufficient self-control to deny myself the sweet pleasure she was offering to me. "No, dearie!" I said, "I'd like it awfully, but I must reserve myself to tonight and you three!" "Oh you good boy" she whispered —then after kissing me again she said in her usual voice "now I'll leave you and will join you presently at tea; I can now get on well till tonight! Oh Jack!, I do hope you'll have me first?" then disappeared.

I found Mrs. Bell and Alice already at the tea table. Alice again blushed on seeing me, and I fancied that Mrs. Bell looked somewhat enquiringly at me. "Where's Maud?" she asked. "I expected to find her here", I replied— "she went on to her room after showing me to mine; here she comes!" And then we chatted gaily. I gave them the latest news from London and they detailed the County gossip to me, for I knew many of the families. And so tea passed, and when we rose I was glad to note that Alice's shyness and restraint had disappeared.

True to her undertaking, Maud drew Alice's arm through hers and led her off into the garden, while I chatted with Mrs. Bell and followed her into her own particular boudoir. As I closed the door she came towards me with open arms and love in her beautiful eyes, drew me to her and kissed me sweetly, whispering "Jack!! it is good of you to come to the help of us poor women—but what can you think of us to ask it!"

I returned her kiss lovingly, then passed my arm round her waist and led her to a settee for two, into which we settled ourselves in delightfully close contact. "There is only one thing I can think, Mrs. Bell", I replied softly as I looked into her eyes— "you, Maud, and Alice are simply angels." She laughed and blushed prettily, then whispered "you called me Helen when you arrived—I want to continue to be Helen to you now that we are going to be so ... so ... intimate!" I drew her to me and tenderly kissed her, and for a moment she rested silent in my embrace.

Presently she freed herself. "I want to talk with you, Jack—you and I have to arrange matters! Maud has told me that you will ... play! now have you anything to suggest?"

"I'd rather leave myself in your hands, Helen darling", I said, noting delightedly her pleasure at my form of address. "I'm sure that you and Maud have discussed matters and that you have some scheme cut and dry. And there is sweet little Alice, who is differently placed to you two—I'm sure you can arrange for her initiation better than I possibly can! But tell me, Helen, is Alice really willing to ... surrender her maiden treasure to me?—it seems incredible!"

"She really is willing, Jack", Mrs. Bell replied; "you have her heart and her love, Jack, and she is quite willing to let you have her body, her maidenhead! And Jack, may I say that I also love you, dear, and willingly give myself to you!" And drawing me to her she kissed me passionately.

I was very touched. "I haven't words to say what I feel, Helen darling", I whispered in her ear, — "but may I have a chance tonight to show you how I appreciate your wonderful kindness and love!"

She blushed prettily. "This is what I want to talk about and to arrange with you, Jack dear", she replied softly. "May I tell you our ideas?"

"Please do!" I answered, and drew her against me so that she could whisper—for I recognized she could whisper what she could not say in the usual way. And to indicate my recognition of the sweet intimacy into which she had now admitted me, my disengaged hand stole towards her corsage and lovingly wandered over her voluptuous bust!

Mrs. Bell began. "You know, Jack, that all the servants sleep in the domestic wing, leaving us along in the house. They cannot see the lights in my room and they know that I sometimes read for hours after I retire—because I am alone!" she added with a blush and smile "By half-past ten the house is quite quiet. My idea is that instead of your visiting us in our own rooms in turn and perhaps attracting attention by the lights, we all should meet in my bedroom, clad only in our "nighties", and that you should work your sweet will on us in the presence of each other. There will then be no jealousies—things will more or less be done on the spur of the moment—and the feeling that each one is assisting the others and contributing by her presence to the piquancy of the proceedings will add zest to our pleasures. How does it strike you?—I see a smile on your lips!"

"I think your idea a most charming one", I replied, looking fondly at her and amorously playing with the swell of her bosom— "may I confess that I know from personal experience how much the pleasure of . . . having a woman . . . is enhanced by the presence of another girl. But our case is so exceptional that I could not refrain from a smile as its peculiarities struck me!"

"In what way?" she asked, somewhat anxiously I thought.

"You will let me use plain words and not beat about the bush?" I enquired.

"Certainly, Jack", she replied with a conscious smile and blush.

"Well, Helen, you and Maud are mother and daughter—not many daughters are ... fucked ... in the sight of their mothers, and fewer mothers still allow their daughters to watch them being fucked! Are you sure you and Maud won't mind? I shall insist on your being stark naked!"

"Quite sure!" Helen replied stoutly—but she coloured violently. I kissed her tenderly.

"It will be awfully delicious!" I said delightedly, and I felt a responsive quiver run through her.

I continued. "Now we come to Alice. To speak plainly, she has to be ravished by me, eh Helen?"

"That's really what it is, Jack!" she replied slowly, blushing deeply.

"Will she agree to be violated in public, so-to-speak,—will she not prefer the privacy of her own room and to lose her maindenhead alone with me?"

"I don't think so, Jack" Helen replied, looking soberly at me; "she is very young and very timid and nervous, and really both Maud and I thought that she she seemed relieved when we told her that we would be present to look after her while she was being ravished!"

"Then, Helen, I think your idea is really splendid and am ready to fall in with it. I would like to make just one suggestion—some one of us should be appointed each evening to direct the proceedings and to say what is to be cone, and the others are to give implicit obedience. Deal the cards round every evening when we meet in your room, and whoever gets the Ace of Spades is to be the Queen or King of that evening."

"Oh Jack! what a lovely idea!" she exclaimed delightedly— "we can have a regular revel or games at every meeting then!"

I kissed her. "I have seen the game played, Helen, and I'm sure you all will love it!" One question more—do we meet this evening?"

She blushed "We thought we might do so, Jack, if you were willing and not too tired after your long journey!"

"The prospect of seeing you in all your naked beauty, Helen, and of making you die of esctacy in my arms would be enough to banish all fatigue did it exist, which it aoes not. So we will meet!" She kissed me rapturously.

"Is Alice to be ... sacrificed ... this evening, or do you propose that she should be saved for to-morrow, and be educated a little by the help of object lessons furnished by you and Maud. What do you think, Helen?"

"We thought we would leave that to you, Jack," she replied—" "we considered that you ought to have the right to choose."

I drew her closely to me. "Then we'll keep Alice for tomorrow night, darling, and I'll devote myself to you and Maud tonight. But we will make Alice show herself to us naked tonight—and as our loving pranks are sure to excite her virgin self, I must claim the privilege of affording her the relief she will crave. Now Helen dear, just one point more; will you mind if I have Maud first, and then you?"

"Of course not, Jack," Helen replied with a smile— "I think you ought to, especially if she wishes it."

"I'm sure she will, for she is so terribly mad with desire!" I said, "the sight of you in my arms, quivering with ecstacy, will probably drive her wild! Besides this, Helen, it will be better for Alice to have you with her when she sees ... fucking ... for the first time!" (Helen kissed me rapturously). "I'll do Maud as soon as I can arrange it—then we'll play for a bit with Alice and utilise her naked charms to excite us—and then, my darling, you and I will have a long sweet fuck!" (Helen kissed me rapturously). "I'll then dissolve the meeting— but I'll slip back to you, and we'll have a sweet time by ourselves! Now, one final kiss, and we'll join the others. Get Maud away and tell her what we have arranged, —I'll entertain Alice; perhaps you'll also tell her that she is to be reserved as tomorrow night's *bonne bouche*, —she then will be more at her ease tonight, and we'll use her to excite us. Now Helen darling!" and after a long passionate kiss, lips on lips, we strolled into the garden. As arranged, Helen soon disappeared with Maud, leaving me with Alice, who at first was very shy and timid—but when she found that I did not touch on the topic of her sacrifice she soon regained her usual easy and charming demeånour. In due course came dinner, then cards and music—and so bed-time was comfortably and happily reached.

CHAPTER TWO

Carefully and ceremoniously we wished each other good night while the servants were removing the cakes and glasses and closing for house. When I was undressed and ready for the fray I glanced at the clock and to my disgust found it was only ten minutes past the hour and that I had twenty horrid minutes to wait. It could not be helped. I got into a comfortable chair and recalled the dinner table with the three ladies in their dainty evening attire—how my eyes dwelt on what they were kind enough to display in the way of bosom—how my prick throbbed at the thought that very soon I should see those bosoms unveiled and bare! Then my thoughts wandered to the sur-

roudning bedrooms and their occupants—I could
imagine Maud dragging off her garments in her
excitement and surveying herself naked in the mirror preparatory to slipping on her only robe—I
could picture Mrs. Bell's agitation as she carefully
prepared herself for the fucking for which she so
longed—and I could almost see Alice as she nervously undressed herself to appear before me clad
in her "nightie" only! At dinner she chattered
away so freely and delightfully and seemed so
much at her ease save for a certain suppressed
excitement that I felt certain she had been told
that her ordeal had been postponed to the following
night and that she therefore was to play the part
chiefly of spectator and Maid of Honour.

At last the clock in the hall chimed the half-
hour; promptly I rose, turned out my lights and
noiselessly slipped into the landing; a thin line of
light indicated Mrs. Bell's room and that the door
was ajar. Into it I went.

Mrs. Bell and Alice were there, sitting together,
their "nighties" on, the most dainty and provoking
garments I ever saw! As I approached them they
both rose. Helen opened her arms to me and clasping me to her she said "Welcome here Jack!" and
kissed me; then pushing me towards the blushing
Alice she said "Now Alice!"—whereupon the sweet
girl threw her arms round me and held up her face
to be kissed. I took her in my arms and pressing
her closely to me I showered hot kisses on her lips

till she gasped for breath, when I released her, and she took refuge alongside of Mrs. Bell again.

Just then Maud appeared, wearing the most ravishing "nightie" I had ever seen—for it was semi-transparent! She kissed us all in turn, then looked inquiringly at her mother.

"Jack dear, we want you to direct the proceedings tonight instead of someone being chosen by the fall of a card—then we shall learn the game better and how to play it!" said Mrs. Bell, looking at me and slightly colouring;—"we'll all promise to do whatever you wish and in the way you wish. Will you be so kind?"

"Why, of course, Helen!" I answered, concealing my joy—for was not I now master of the situation!

"And if you don't mind, Jack, will you be content with Maud and me only tonight, and let Alice see for herself how the game is played; then tomorrow we will put her at your disposal!, added Mrs. Bell, passing her arm round Alice's waist protectingly as the blushing girl nestled closely against her.

"Why, certainly, Helen dear!" I replied with a smile to Alice; but I suppose that Alice is willing to take her part in everything else that we may play at?"

Mrs. Bell turned to Alice. "What do you say, dear?" she asked lovingly.

Alice hesitated for a moment, then colouring

deeply replied in a low voice "Yes, Auntie, if you wish it!"

"There's your answer Jack!", said Mrs. Bell with a smile. "Now my Lord, your handmaidens await your commands!"

"Alice, dear, come and sit on my knees!" I said. Hesitatingly Alice left her Aunt's sheltering arm and gently placed herself on my knees, sitting so that she faced Maud and her mother. I slipped my left arm round her to hold her in position and lovingly kissed her. It was a delicious sensation to feel her soft weight on my thighs and to note the little tremors that pulsated through her, for she now was fairly quivering with excitement.

"Helen, will you now show yourself to us?" I said—" Maud, dear please strip your Mother stark naked, and then come here to look at her with us!"

"Oh! Jack!, no, no," protested Helen, flushing furiously. But Maud delightedly seized her. "Stand up, Mummy!" she cried as she set to work to unbutton Mrs. Bell's "nightie". Slowly and reluctantly Helen complied; quickly Maud pulled the "nightie" off her and threw it on the bed—and Mrs. Bell stood naked in front of us, one arm and hand in front of her breasts while with the other hand she covered her cunt!

I felt Alice thrill! I glanced at her—she was rosy red, but her eyes were rivetted on her Aunt's naked figure. Maud remained by her Mother as if expecting further orders—I could see that she was quivering with suppressed excitement.

"Maud, pull your Mother's hands away and clasp them together at the back of her head—and then come here!" I commanded.

"No Jack!, no!" pleaded Helen, who evidently was reluctant to expose her cunt to our gaze. But Maud slipped behind her, gripped her wrists in her strong young arms and pulling them backwards she placed them in the desired position, and quickly joined Alice and me, standing behind my chair her eyes glittering with something very like lust!

In silence we three gazed at Helen—the broken breathing of the two girls betraying their suppressed excitement! Helen naked was certainly a thrilling spectacle—her flushd face, her glorious figure, her wonderful breasts heaving in her agitation, her splendidly round thighs and legs, her grandly swelling hips and haunches, and the bewitching forest of close curling silky hair that clustered over and concealed her cunt!

"Jack! isn't she glorious!" whispered Maud in glowing admiration. I nodded. "Make Mother turn slowly round, Jack, so that we can see her from all points and in profile!" whispered Maud again breathlessly. A quick flush told me that Helen had heard her daughter's suggestion. "Please, Helen!" I said gently,— "very slowly, please!" Reluctantly Helen complied, affording us the most charming succession of views of her magnificent naked self.

When she was in full profile I made her stand still —the sight of her in this position was simply wonderful, the sweep and spring of her back and bottom, the curve of her belly, her proud upstanding breasts with their saucy nipples, and the glorious bush of hairs—it simply fascinated us and I could feel my prick beginning to stiffen and began to wonder if Alice noticed it! After gazing our fill I made Helen continue her revolving—but stopped her again to revel in the view of her splendid buttocks and haunches and her plump thighs. Then starting her again I allowed her to complete the round, and again she faced us, now visibly trembling with apprehension and shame!

"Go and kiss her, girls!" I whispered. Up sprang Alice—simultaneously she and Maud seized Mrs. Bell and smothered her with their ardent kisses. It was a sweet sight to watch—but time was valuable and so I joined the group and rescuing Helen from the excited girls I installed her on my knees, naked as she was, showering burning kisses on her quivering lips, while my hands sought her glorious breasts and squeezed them.

"Now Maud, its your turn!" I said; "strip dear and how us your naked beauties. Help her to take off her 'nightie', Alice!"

In a trice Maud stood naked before her Mother and me, a lovely vision of voluptuous slenderness. To me the sight was familiar, but to her mother and to Alice it was a revelation which struck them dumb with admiration. Helen's broken breathing told me how much the sight of her daughter's naked loveliness was affecting her, while Alice simply thrilled with undisguised pleasure, her eyes dwelling almost wonderingly on the glorious wealth of golden fluffy hair that grew on Maud's Mount of Venus and sheltered her cunt. We made Maud turn herself slowly round, just as her Mother did, revelling in the spectacle of her bewitching slenderness; and when she again faced us, her cheeks suffused with blushes, I stealthily watched Helen's eyes as they wandered over her daughter's voluptuously naked body and her delicious breasts and her golden haired cunt!

"Haven't you seen her like this before?" I whispered in her ear. Helen blushed. "No!" she replied softly— "Maud was quite a little thing when I last undressed her—now, well Jack, I'm beginning to wish I was a man, for her sake!"—and she laughed wickedly, while Alice who was standing just behind us, leaning on the back of our chair, broke into a ripple of amused girlish mirthful laughter.

"Then you can appreciate what my sensations are, dear!" said as I amorously played with her breasts— "I can guess them, Jack, by the mutinous movements of something I am sitting on!" Helen replied as she moved herself provokingly on my knees, smiling significantly at me.

It was only too true! The sight of her glorious

nakedness, so quickly followed by the display of Maud's voluptuous charms, the inflammatory influence of our close contact and arising from my handling of her breasts (her cunt I did not dare to touch at the moment) all set me on fire! My prick was like a rod of iron! It was full time to have Maud!

I glanced over my shoulder at Alice. She was still intently gazing at Maud, and evidently very excited by her naked beauty. Her eyes were gleaming, her lips partly open, while her bosom throbbed and heaved. She evidently was dominated by intense curiosity which for the time being overpowered her maidenly instincts and training, and some subtle instinct (probably sexual) told her that a crisis was approaching.

"Helen!" I whispered loudly enough for Maud and Alice to hear, "I must have Maud!—do you mind?" Maud blushed prettily, but Alice became crimson as she glanced quickly at me.

"Do, Jack!" Helen replied, kissing me ardently —then she rose so as to set me free. "Come, Alice," she added, reseating herself and pointing to her lap, on which Alice instantly installed herself, quivering with suppressed eagerness. Helen kissed her affectionately and whispered something in her ear that I could not catch but which made Alice colour still more furiously.

In an instant I was naked, my prick standing stiff and rampant in magnificent erection! Maud's eyes glistened joyfully at the sight, but Alice shrank back, startled, in Helen's arms, exclaiming "Oh! oh! Auntie!" her eyes widely dilating with surprise and alarm! "Come here, Jack," said Helen quietly, as she passed her hands caressingly and re-assuringly over Alice. I slipped an arm round Maud, and the pair of us went up together to Helen's chair an stood in front of and close to her and the still startled Alice. "Now look again, dear!" said Helen softly as she pointed to my prick. Timidly Alice did so, flushing a rosy red, her astonished eyes travelling from the threatening rubicond head along the shaft to its root in my forest of hairs, under which my dangling balls were clearly visible, the sight of which evidently filled her with wonder and amazement. With silent curiosity we watched Alice as she gazed on the masculine organ which was so shortly to be lodged in her virgin cunt, and we wondered as to what thoughts were then flashing through her mind at the sight of the instrument of her approaching violation.

Presently Alice drew a deep breath and hid her face against Helen's shoulder, a tremulous wriggle passing through her as she did so! Our eyes met Helen's in an amused smile—Had Alice's sexual excitement at the sight of my prick proved too much for her?—had she spent? But the very idea that Alice's maiden cunt was quivering in ecstacy set Maud and me on fire. "Come, darling!" I exclaimed—and quickly I led her to Helen's bed, which was covered with a plum-coloured counterpane well calculated to set off our nudity—and on it Maud hastily extended herself on her back!

"Quick, Alice! wait a moment, Jack!" cried Helen, as she hurriedly rose, and slipping an arm round the flushed trembling and wildly excited girl she brought Alice to the bedside. Maud's legs were now widely parted to accommodate me, and her golden haired cunt was in full view, its pouting coral lips being clearly visible through the cluster of fluffy golden curls. "Look, dear!", whispered Helen to Alice, indicating Maud's cunt with her finger— "isn't it lovely!" Alice's eyes gleamed as they glanced from Maud's cunt to my impatient prick, intently watching our every movement. "Go on, Jack!" said Helen softly. Quickly I placed myself in position between Maud's legs, and let myself down on to her breasts; and as her arms closed lovingly round me, I brought my prick to bear against the lips of her throbbing excited cunt and gently forced it in! "Look, Alice, look!" whispered Helen excitedly, Alice's eyes dilating with astonishment as she saw how easily Maud's cunt engulfed my prick! Soon it was buried in Maud till our hairs intermingled! "Oh! Jack! . . . darling!" Maud murmured ecstatically with half closed eyes, as after showering burning kisses on her sweet lips I began to fuck her! Instantly she threw her legs across my loins and strained me against her breasts with her strong young arms. "Watch them, darling!" whis-

pered Helen eagerly her voice betraying her own
agitation at the sight. But the injunction was un-
necessary. Alice's eyes were rivetted on our quivering, wriggling, heaving naked bodies, and not a
single movement passed unnoticed! Soon mutual
ecstasy began to steal over us!—wilder and fiercer
became my down-thrustings, madder and more
frenzied became Maud's wriggles and plunges
under me. Then the blissful climax was reached—
an indescribable convulsion swept through both of
us—"Ah! ... ah! ... A-H-H-!!" ejaculated Maud
brokenly as she felt herself inundated with the
boiling torrent that I frantically shot from me as I
spent rapturously into her! For a moment or two
we lay rigid, locked in the closest and sweetest of
embraces—then we collapsed into temporary for-
getfulness of everything but the heavenly bliss we
had tasted in each others arms, the echoes of which
were still thrilling through us! Alice had witnessed
a fuck!

When I had recovered myself and remembered
my surroundings I looked cautiously round for Hel-
en and Alice. I found they had returned to the
chair. Helen, still naked, was seated in it, and Alice,
still in her "nightie" was on her lap, but she had
coiled herself up and had twisted herself round so
as to be lying face to face with Helen, tightly
clasped bosom against bosom in her arms. Her
attitude had somehow pulled her "nightie" tightly
across her bottom, and revealed so delicious an

outline that I involuntarily quivered with pleasure! This quiver aroused Maud, who dreamily opened her eyes; as they met mine a smile of heavenly satisfaction irradiated her countenance—her lips met mine and we exchanged long passionate kisses expressive of our gratitude for the divine raptures we had communicated to each other.

"Look at your Mother and Alice!" I whispered softly. Maud looked and broke into a merry laugh, which made Helen and Alice start up almost guiltily; and as we slowly slipped out of each other's embrace and rose from Helen's bed, they came to meet us, blushing consciously. Maud rushed into her Mother's arms murmuring "Oh Mummy darling!" while Helen responded "Oh Maud dear! oh you happy girl!" as they kissed each other passionately. I held out my arms silently to Alice, who timidly slipped into my embrace and let me kiss her lips. "Darling!' did we please you?" I whispered with a twinkle in my eye. She blushed crimson, averted her eyes, but remained silent; whereupon I added "never mind, dear, you'll tell me better tomorrow night!" whereupon she quivered nervously. Then to my utter surprise she raised herself on tiptoe, turned her blushing face to me and whispered very softly in a voice full of emotion "Kiss me again, Jack, and promise to be kind to me tomorrow when my time comes! "My darling!" I exclaimed, strangely moved,—and again clasping

46

her to me I kissed her passionately over and over again!

Helen's voice interrupted us. "Jack, you can get to your room through that door, its open tonight; Alice dear, come with us!" The three women disappeared into Helen's bathroom, and acting on her hint I slipped into my room and indulged in a most welcome ablution and purification of my organs; then feeling greatly refreshed by the operation I, still naked, returned to Helen's room just as she, also naked, came in alone from her bathroom.

Having the room to ourselves we rushed into each others arms and kissed each other tenderly; the "feel" of her flesh against mine was simply exquisite, and I thrilled to think that before long she would be locked in my arms in the closest of embraces!

"Jack! it was just wonderful!" she murmured; "Maud says it was the best ... fuck ... she ever had!" "And what did Alice think of it, Helen?" I asked eagerly. She laughed. "Alice is absolutely staggered, Jack! In her wildest and wickedest moments she never imagined anything like what she has now seen; the sight of you and Maud in each others arms excited her terribly—and when the wonderful finale was reached, I took her away and made her sit on my lap in the fashion you saw, for I am sure that otherwise she would have used her hands to get relief for her feelings! I was very bad myself!" she added with a conscious blush. "Did you spend, Helen?", I asked mischievously. "No, no, Jack!" she responded smilingly, "but I was hard put to control myself!" "Do you think Alice spent?" I asked somewhat anxiously. "No, Jack, I know she didn't, but she admitted to Maud in the bathroom just now that she very nearly did!" "Where is she now?" I enquired. "In my bathroom with Maud," Helen replied. I thought it as well to leave the two girls together and I expect Alice is plying Maud with questions! I think you will have the sweetest of pupils tomorrow night, Jack dear!", she added with a smile— "I am looking forward to it with very pleasurable expectations."

"When the girls join us, Helen, we'll make Alice show us herself naked," I said; "We'll play with her and tease her and excite her again and then I'll satisfy her desires and cravings in a way she will think is just heavenly. By that time I shall be ready to fuck you, my darling" (she kissed me rapturously) "a good, long and slow fuck?" (another passionate kiss). "After that we'll dissolve the meeting—but I'll slip back to you through that door, it won't be midnight, so we can have a long sweet time together by ourselves in your bed and in each others arms" (more passionate kisses) "here they come!"

As we disengaged ourselves from our sweet embrace Maud and Alice with arms interlaced emerged from Helen's bathroom, Maud looking radiant, while Alice's face simply beamed with happiness; for she had now witnessed an act of fucking, and her maiden dread had been chased away by the sight of our rapturous transports. Also she had the pleasurable knowledge that she would presently be watching Helen in my arms; and so when Maud sank into an easy chair Alice settled herself down comfortably on Maud's lap and smiled brightly at us.

But her happy complacency was about to be rudely disturbed! I had drawn Helen again on to my knees and was playing with her glorious breasts while she exchanged a laughing badinage with Maud which greatly amused Alice. Presently my right hand slipped down over Helen's stomach, and after gently tickling her naval it descended towards her cunt, which up to now I had not yet touched. Hastily she stopped me. "No, Jack, you mustn't!" she exclaimed somewhat shamefacedly, "you mustn't touch me there!—I'm too excited!—I should go off." Maud and Alice shook with silent laughter, then Maud said mischievously "Hurry up, Jack, or you'll lose the train," which provoked further laughter in which Helen and I joined. "I've got at least twenty minutes yet, Maud," I replied, "I'm not built on the revolver principle and keep on firing—I've got to load my gun again and must not hurry the process or I will not be able to do your Mother justice!"

"Twenty minutes!" exclaimed Maud dolefully, —"what shall we do all that time?"

"Let me see," I replied. "I am Director tonight! I think that we cannot fill up the time better than by putting Alice through some of her paces; come, Alice dear, slip out of your nightie and show us yourself naked, to begin with!"

The happy smile fled from Alice's face and a look of dismay succeeded it as she cried "Oh no, Jack!, please no!" "An excellent idea Jack," cried Maud delightedly—"come Alice, let me undress you!"— and she commenced to unbutton Alice's "nightie." "No, no, don't Maud!" cried Alice, resisting stoutly, but Helen rushed to Maud's assistance. Between them they got the "nightie" off Alice, then each seized a wrist and gently forced her to stand in front of me stark naked!

Delightedly did my eyes rove over Alice's shrinking naked body. Helen held her firmly by one wrist, Maud by the other; her arms were thus forced away from her sides and so allowed her lovely outlines the fullest display,—and as her hands were captive she could not hide her most private parts from my eager gaze. Her skin was like milk! She had the loveliest little breasts I ever saw, so sweetly full and ripe, and so deliciously saucy! The little pink nipples pointing outwards; while the exquisitely subtle curves of her figure as it swept inwards to her waist and then swelled outwards over her hips and on to her legs were dreams

50

of beauty! Her thighs were gloriously plump and round, and melted into the daintiest of calves with slender ankles and tiny arched feet! Her beautifully rounded belly was surmounted with a large and deep navel and sloped gently down to its junction with her thighs, her Hill of Venus being unusually large and prominent and fleshy, and covered with a delicious tangle of closely curling silky hair, through which the delicate pink lips of her cunt were visible! She was just the daintiest, sweetest, prettiest little maiden one could imagine,—and her delicious young freshness crowned everything!

I sat still, simply enraptured! Before me stood a wonderful trio—Helen and Maud, tall, splendidly voluptuous, stark naked, holding between them Alice in her dainty nakedness, her face suffused with deep blushes which surged down to her dear little breasts, as half-laughingly and half-nervously she begged to be let loose.

"Bring her here to me," I said at last, separating my legs widely an act that seemed really to alarm Alice and compelled Helen and Maud to use gentle force; and soon the naked struggling girl stood between my thighs held firmly there by Helen and Maud, now deeply interested in the proceedings. "Don't touch me, Jack! please don't!" begged Alice, now quite frightened and trembling violently with flushed face and cast down eyes! I placed my hands just behind her hips, noting delightedly how she squirmed when I touched her, while the sight of her palpitating bosom and heaving breasts began to re-animate my prick!

"Alice dear," I said softly, "You're behaving very naughtily, and you are breaking your promise to do everything I might wish if you were let off from doing one special thing tonight! Do you think we would hurt you, dear? On the contrary, we're going to give you the sweetest time you've ever had, and prepare you for tomorrow! Now darling, take courage! Come and kiss me, and smile again!"

I pressed her coaxingly towards me as I spoke; for a brief moment Alice stood irresolute—then she raised her eyes looked lovingly at me, smiled trustfully, and, yielding to the gentle pressure of my hands, she allowed herself to be drawn forward till she was resting against me. Then she held up her lips to me to be kissed. "My darling!" I whispered passionately, clasping her in my arms, and pressing her warm soft body against mine. I kissed her over and over again!

"Now you can let go of her hands, Helen, for Alice has become a good girl again!" I said with a smile, as I arranged Alice on my knees, retaining her in that position with my left arm and keeping my right in readiness to feel her naked person—the sweet warmth and pressure of her bottom on my prick beginning to infuse fresh life to my somewhat limp organ. Helen, meanwhile, had settled herself again in her chair and faced me; she took Maud on her lap and then began to play with Maud's lovely breasts and generally to feel her, all the time looking significantly at me.

I took the hint and said to Alice, "Look at those two, dear, it's a pretty game, isn't it!" Alice coloured vividly, then laughed uneasily, but watched Helen and Maud attentively.

Helen then exclaimed "Don't you know this game, Jack?—its only 'Follow my Leader'! I'm leader!—whatever I do to Maud you are to do to Alice!"

"Oh! Auntie!" exclaimed Alice, considerably startled at the idea. She turned and looked at me inquiringly.

I smiled encouragingly and asked "Shall we play, dear?"

Her colour rose, she hesitated, then whispered "Yes, if you wish it, Jack!"—then laughed gaily as if amused by her audacity!

Helen commenced by kissing Maud on her lips; I did the same to Alice. Helen next placed her hand just below Maud's breasts and felt her all over her stomach, roving backwards and forwards at her sweet will, sometimes going perilously near Maud's cunt. I followed suit, revelling in the feel of Alice's firm, soft and springy flesh and sweet skin, smiling mischievously at her as she winced when my hand neared her cunt. Helen then devoted her attention to Maud's hips, haunches, buttocks and thighs, her hand dwelling lovingly on the plumper and fleshier parts, which she gently squeezed and caressed,

53

visiting them again and again. Delightedly, I did the same to Alice, who now began to show signs of agitation. When I followed Helen's lead and forced my hand between Alice's plump thighs, so closely prssed together, and began to luxuriate in her rich, juicy, smooth flesh (my hand travelling dangerously near to her cunt) she ejaculated confusedly, "Oh Jack! ... Oh Jack! ..."—then laughed nervously at her own discomfiture!

Helen here refreshed herself by kissing Maud, a proceeding I was not slow to follow with Alice and which she appreciated.

"Shall we go on, Jack?" then asked Helen.

"Shall we, Alice?" I queried with a smile.

"I'm quite willing, Jack," she replied with a blush, then added laughingly "only Auntie is getting very daring!"

"I'll pay you out, my beauty!" retorted Helen as she joined in the laugh: "Now Maud!"—and she began to tickle Maud's navel, making her wriggle prettily with the titillation.

I applied my finger to Alice's navel. "Oh! Jack dear!" she exclaimed with heightening colour and increasing agitation as she began squirming and writhing and twisting herself about, joining nevertheless in Helen's triumphant laughter.

"Now we'll try something else!" said Helen mischievously—and to Alice's dismay she gently attacked Maud's breasts, keeping her eyes on Alice! Delightedly, I followed suit, and before Alice could interpose her free hand my eager hand had flown up to her bosom and had captured her left breast! Jack!" cried Alice, flushing furiously as she seized my hand and endeavoured to drag it away from its tempting prey, nevertheless laughing (though somewhat uneasily) at her complete discomfiture— but she found me too strong for her.

When I whispered gently, "You must submit dear—this is part of your preparation for tomorrow," she loyally, though reluctantly, accepted the position and surrendered her sweet twin globes to my tender mercies, her agitated breathing and restless movements indicating her perturbation and emotion at my hand's invasion of her maiden breasts!

Helen and Maud had suspended their game— that is to say, Maud was still on her Mother's lap with her mother's arm round her, and Helen's right hand was still playing with her daughter's beautiful breasts, but they evidently found it much more interesting and exciting to watch Alice's first experience with kind but inquisitive male fingers! The shock of feeling a man's hand on her maiden breasts had to a certain extent died away, and Alice was now lying resting on me, her right arm clasping me round my neck, her left hanging by her side, the hand tightly gripping the chair rail—the distant expression in her eyes as they idly fell on objects without seeming to see them, indicating her intense absorption in the sensations of the moment as she felt her virgin breasts stroked, caressed, and squeezed by my eager though gentle hands! For me it was a delicious occupation! Alice's little bubbies were so firm, and yet so springy and fleshy and, above all, so virginal, that my fingers absolutely revelled in their feel; and for some considerable time I could not bring myself to relinquish them!

At last, with a strong effort, I tore my hand away, and sliding it down to her navel, I brought Alice back to a consciousness of her surroundings and whereabouts by gently tickling that sensitive part of her! As her eyes resumed their duties they met those of Helen and Maud, beaming sympathy and signalling encouragement, and she smiled gratefully at them as she roused herself, murmuring, "Oh Jack dear, don't!" At this juncture Helen caught my eye, then slowly ran her hand from Maud's breasts over her stomach and down to her cunt, where her fingers began gently to pull and play with the lovely tangle of fluffy golden hair that clustered there! Alice became scarlet! It had never ocurred to her that her cunt was to be felt, and when my hand followed Helen's lead and slipped downwards over her belly she clutched my wrist wildly, threw one thigh closely over the other so as to defend the approach, and exclaimed agitatedly, "No, no darling!—no, Jack dear!—you mustn't touch me there!"—then kissed me frenziedly as if to dissuade me!

I let my hand remain in her grip and said quietly

and soothingly, "You must play the game, dear!—besides that, what did I tell you just now?" She looked questioningly and imploringly at me with eyes full of dismay! I drew her to me and kissed her lovingly, whispering "Cannot you trust yourself to me, darling?"

For reply she nestled her soft cheek against mine, and then murmured, "Jack, must you do it?"

"Yes, Alice dear!" I replied softly—"and tomorrow you will thank me for insisting!" For a moment she hesitated,—then without a word she released my wrist and slowly and reluctantly unlocked her thighs!

"May I, darling?" I asked gently.

"Yes, dear!" she replied softly and tremulously, then pressed her cheek still more closely against mine till our lips nearly rested on each other—she tightened her clasp round my neck as if to nerve her for the ordeal, while her eyes sought Helen's and rested appealing on her as if asking for her sympathy and guidance!

I decided that this time I would invade Alice's maiden cunt by the valley formed by her closely pressed thighs, at the head of which I should find her Hill of Venus, its unusual size and prominence being intensified by her sitting position—which made the tangle of curly silky hairs stand out like a bush. Accordingly I did so. To Alice's surprise, I dropped my hand lightly on her thighs, about half way down them, then it travelled upwards between their soft smooth surface till it arrived at her shrubbery, when (following Helen's lead) I played amorously with her hairs, now pulling them gently, now twining them round my fingers, now softly brushing them—a proceeding that seemed to excite Alice judging from the way in which she agitated her bottom on my knees! After a little of this toying I proceeded with forefinger and thumb to explore the region covered by her hairs, pressing and squeezing its delicious soft springy flesh, but carefully avoiding the tender sensitive opening—till Alice's involuntary wrigglings and squirmings and the increasing agitation of her bosom told me that she had arrived at the condition of erotic sexual excitement that I desired. Then I gently applied my forefinger to the lips of Alice's tender maiden cunt!

"Oh! Jack!" she cried, drawing herself back hurriedly, as if to escape from my finger, which, however, not only retained, but improved its position, and now began to move along the delicate slit—creating the most exquisite tickling sensations, which Alice evidently enjoyed! She clutched me tighter than ever round my neck, she quivered voluptously, she brought her lips to bear upon mine and began to kiss me ardently—and where my finger inserted itself into the virgin recesses of her cunt and commenced to agitate itself seductively, Alice fairly lost control of herself and surrendered herself unrestrainedly to the gratification of her sexual desires and her newly born erotic lust!

I glanced triumphantly at Helen—but to my astonishment, she was busily engaged with Maud! Her hand was buried well between Maud's thighs, and her finger was evidently hard at work in her daughter's cunt, for Maud was wriggling and quivering and jerking herself about in extreme lascivious frenzy—and it was clear that the ecstatic crisis was at hand. The piquant spectacle of Helen frigging Maud—of a mother frigging her daughter was too much for me!—I redoubled my ministrations to Alice and set to work deliberately to make her spend! She and Maud were by now far too excitedly absorbed in their own voluptuous sensations to pay any attention to each other. "Jack! Oh! Darling!" gasped Alice almost incoherently as, wriggling violently, she jerked herself madly forward as if to encourage my finger to more furious exertion in her cunt.

"Oh! Mummy! oh Mummy dear! . . . keep on! . . . keep on!" ejaculated Maud wildly in her lascivious frenzy!

Seeing that Alice was now on the verge of erotic collapse I attached her virgin clitoris and furiously tickled it! "Ha! . . . ha! . . . ha!! . . . " she gasped— then, with an indescribable spasmodic paroxysm, she spent voluptuously, bedewing my finger with her creamy virgin essence.

Almost simultaneously Maud went off with a

half-strangled cry of "Ah! ... Mummy darling!!" clinging frantically to Helen as the spasms of her sexual rapture vibrated through her and quenched the fires of her lust!

Maud was the first to come to herself which she did very soon. She kissed her Mother gratefully, and they both came across to me to welcome Alice back "from the angels," she being still unconscious! I cautiously drew my finger out of her cunt, and with the air of the victor I exhibited it to them; wet, glistening and sticky with Alice's maiden spend, the display provoking them to silent laughter! Just then Alice moved herself uneasily, then drew a long breath and dreamily opened her eyes. As they met Helen's, the recollection of her whereabouts and of what she had been doing flashed on her! She blushed violently, sprang to her feet, and buried her face in her hands, murmuring shamedly, "Oh Auntie!, Auntie!"

Helen took her affectionately in her arms and said, "There is nothing to be ashamed of, darling— we've not come to scold but to congratulate you on your debut!"

Overjoyed, Alice kissed her gratefully, embraced Maud, then threw herself into my arms (I had then risen) murmuring "Oh darling! Darling!" But my prick had been so irritated and inflamed by the movements of her soft warm bottom on it that it stood rampant and stiff and stark!

"Oh, look at poor Jack!" cried Maud as she

pointed to it—"And poor Mother too, who has not yet had anything. Wait half a minute for us Jack. Come, Alice!" and the two girls rushed off into Helen's bathroom. Hurriedly Helen and I performed our ablutions, mad for each other, then I placed her on her bed, put a hard cushion under her bottom, separated her thighs, and sat by her, impatiently waiting for the girls' re-appearance—the while feasting my eyes on Helen's beautiful cunt now so gloriously displayed, while Helen gently stroked my raging prick!

Very soon the girls hurried in, beaming with pleasurable excitement and anticipation. "Now Jack! into Mother!" cried Maud.

I needed no encouragement! In a trice I was on the bed and between Helen's legs, and was just about to plunge my prick into her cunt when Alice innocently intervened! "Please Jack, may I feel it?" she asked.

In spite of ourselves we all laughed! "Yes, dear!" I replied, "You may feel me, and you may put me into Helen!" The touch of her soft maiden hand nearly made my tool burst with pleasure. "Now, Alice dear!" I cried as I let myself down on to Helen. Holding my prick in her dainty fingers, Alice cleverly guided its head into Helen's throbbing and expectant cunt and delightedly watched it as it disappeared inch by inch, Helen all the time whinnying with the rapture of again feeling a male organ lodged in her! But we both were too ardent

61

and excited to take our pleasure slowly, as we had intended! As soon as Helen found me well up her cunt and felt my arms close firmly round her till her breasts flattened against me, she began to agitate herself under me wildly, wriggling and writhing, jerking herself about, moving her legs restlessly—sometimes stretching them, at other times twisting them round me! To prolong her blissful transports, I lay on her as motionless and as rigid as I possibly could, leaving her to really fuck herself, in the hope that her furious movements would provoke her into spending quickly— and so it happened, for soon she strained me passionately to her and jogging herself upwards violently she spent rapturously, ejaculating brokenly "Oh my darling! ... my dar ... ling ... ," with such voluptuous quivers and tremors that she nearly sent me spending also! I was, however, able to resist the sweet temptation, and when her spasms of pleasure ceased to thrill through her, I began to fuck her delightedly slowly; but another cyclone of sexual passion and just swept through Helen, and again she began to riot under me in furious plungings and curvettings, her head rolling from side to side in the vehemence of her desires! I could not any longer control myself, I let myself go and rammed fiercely into her! Helen responded by jerking herself madly upwards as if to meet my down thrusts! Then ensued a veritable cyclone of heaves from her and fierce ramming thrusts from me in the wildest fury—then the ecstatic crisis overtook me, and frantically I spent into Helen, she receiving my boiling tribute with the most voluptuous and rapturous transports of bliss as she herself yielded to nature and spent madly in thrills of delight!

For some little while we lay lost to the world, tightly casped in each other's arms—then slowly we came to; our lips met in tender kisses, and then I slowly drew my prick out of Helen's cunt and rose. Maud and Alice at once fell on her and kissed her passionately—then Maud whispered something in her Mother's ear and promptly Helen rose and, with a loving glance at me, she disappeared with the two girls. I slipped into my room and quickly performed a most necessary and welcome ablution; then I put on my night attire as a hint to Maud and Alice that the seance was closed.

Before long they all returned and following my lead they put on their "nighties" ... then Helen said "Now my dears, it is time for bed. Good night, Jack dear! Oh how good you have been to all of us!" and tenderly she kissed me.

"Good night, Jack! And thank you so much!" said Maud archly as she kissed me.

Alice said nothing, but when our lips met in a passionate kiss she breathed, "Oh my darling!" Then we retired to our separate rooms.

CHAPTER THREE

In about fifteen minutes Helen noiselessly opened my door and said softly, "Jack!" and promptly I went into her room, still naked. She was still in her nightie; I begged her to take it off, and again she stood before me in all her glorious nudity! I pointed to her bed, and soon we lay on it side by side, my left arm 'round her, whil emy right hand, after playing a little with her lovely breasts, wandered down to her cunt.

Presently I took hold of her and gently conducted it to my prick, which still lay limp and inert. With a loving smile she began to play with it, sometimes stroking it, sometimes caressing it, feeling my balls and pulling my hairs, evidently delighted in her occupation. Needless to say, it was not long before my organ began to show signs of returning life, and soon it was in fair erection again.

"Why Jack! You're ready again!" she whispered admiringly as she continued to play and fondle it

"Yes, darling!, thanks to you!" I murmured with a kiss of gratitude—"and you?" Helen blushed prettily, then wriggled lasciviously as my finger slipped into the warm and moist interior of her cunt—no answer was necessary as her eyes proclaimed my readiness.

My prick now was in full erection! I whispered to Helen "put it into you, darling!" She looked uncomprehendingly at me! I whispered again "straddle across me, dear, . . . that's right, now take hold of my prick and put it into your cunt yourself . . . now sink down on it, and let yourself take it all in . . . slowly darling, that's the way . . . now lie on me!"

In surprise and wondering astonishment Helen obeyed, hesitatingly at first—but when she began to impale herself on my rampant prick, she comprehended the sweet manvever and lent herself almost too energetically to it; but soon she had my prick stiffly lodged up her cunt, then she lowered herself gently on to me murmuring "Oh Jack! How delicious! How heavenly!" as with a few voluptuous wriggles she settled herself luxuriously on me, her eyes sparkling with delight as my arms closed round her and imprisoned her! As for me I was in the seventh heaven of bliss as I lay under Helen, clasping her luscious and palpitating naked body in my arms with my prick engulfed in her moist, warm, and throbbing cunt! Her full large breasts lay sweetly on my chest, our eyes looked straight into each other's, her ripe lips rested on mine and our breaths mingled as we exchanged long passionate and burning kisses in our mutual rapture! And so we lay silent for a while, absorbed in the exquisite sensations of the moment!

"Am I to do anything, Jack?" Helen presently whispered.

"Not just now, darling," I replied softly—"Just keep as you are and rest yourself on me, lie limply, dear, and let me enjoy your delicious weight on me! We'll have a sweet talk, all the time tasting each other—then when we can no longer wait you'll have to ... fuck me!—and yourself on me!—you'll have to do all the work this time!"

"Oh Jack!" Helen murmured delightedly, her eyes sparkling again with pleasurable anticipation —and involuntarily she began to agitate herself voluptuously on me. Quickly I passed my hands along her back to her bottom, and gripping her gloriously plump fleshy buttocks, I checked her movements whispering "Steady, Helen darling! Lie still, dear—or you'll set us both off!—let us prolong this delicious agony, and when we let ourselves go our pleasure will be all the greater".

"Oh Jack! I couldn't help it!" Helen murmured faintly, then she suddenly caught her breath, her eyes half-closed and an indescribable tremor quivered through her. She had provoked herself into spending! I patted her bottom tenderly. Then she raised her humid eyes to mine, and kissed me rapturously as she whispered "Oh Jack, that was lovely! Now I will lie quiet and be a good girl!" And again she voluptuously settled herself on me.

I transferred my hands from her bottom to her breasts and fondly caressed Helen's delicious bubbies as they rested sweetly on me, and again we lay silent for a while.

Presently she whispered in my ear "Jack, are you going to . . . to ravish Alice this evening?"

"I think so, darling!" I replied, "Provided, of course, that she is willing to let me have her! Has she said anything to you?"

"No," Helen answered, "But I'm sure she wishes you to . . . fuck her, dear! The sight of first Maud and then me in your arms excited her terribly—you should have heard her questions when we were in the bathroom,—I think she would have liked to have been ravished there and then!"

"Then she shall be deflowered this evening!" I said—"The very idea of holding her tight in my arms while I force my prick into her maiden cunt is enough to . . . make me spend now!" Helen kissed me passionately, and began to jog herself gently on me!

"Steady, darling!" I whispered warningly as I

soothed her. "Alice has a largish cunt, has she not?"

"Yes," Helen replied with an arch smile, "Alice has quite a large cunt—as large as mine!" she added with a conscious blush and an involuntary wriggle. "You'll hurt her very little, I fancy, Jack, and it will be sweet to see her in your arms, especially when she feels herself inundated for the first time with warm love juice!" and her eyes glistened as she amorously kissed me. Then she whispered in sudden agitation "Jack! I must . . .! —may I, darling?"

I nodded with a loving smile and folded my arms again 'round Helen so as to hold her firmly against me. Again she whispered, this time flushing deeply, "Darling, promise to lie quite still, and let me do . . . everything!" and again I nodded smilingly.

Voluptuously, Helen arranged herself on me, kissed me tenderly, laid her cheek against mine and, gripping me tightly, she began to jog herself up and down on my prick, agitating herself on me in the most delicious way and making me fairly thrill with delight! At first she moved herself slowly and rythmically—but before long the increasing flutters of her bosom clasped so tightly against me, and her broken breathing indicated her rapidly growing lust; soon she was wriggling furiously on me, her bottom heaving and tossing wildly as she worked herself up and down on my stiff and ram-

69

pant prick with riotously rapid movements. Soon the blissful crisis overtook her—a convulsive quiver thrilled thrrough her, and with a half-strangled inarticulate cry Helen spent rapturously and collapsed, her whole body pulsating as the spasm of pleasure shot through her!

True to my promise, I lay absolutely rigid and motionless—but I had to exercise all my powers of self-control to prevent myself from joining her in spending!—and as she lay quiet on me, I gradually regained complete hold over myself again. Then I whispered in her ear "Go on again, darling!" Helen instantly roused herself from her semi-swoon, and soon she was again raging wildly on me, wriggling furiously and ramming herself down on my prick in the wildest erotic excitement! Then, for the second time, she spent blissfully, quivering voluptuously in my arms in the throes of her ecstasy! Again I allowed her to lie quiet till she could collect herself —and then I whispered, "Now, darling, we'll finish together!" As if stimulated by the knowledge that her excited cunt was now about to receive the blissful injection Helen clasped me more tightly than ever to her, kissed me passionately and set to work to fuck me (I really cannot describe her movements more truly!). It did not take her long to break down my defense—and I was a willing victim! With long furious strokes of her wildly agitated bottom she worked herself up and down on my now raging prick—then, when my involuntary and uncontrollable quivers told her that she had overcome my stubborn resistance, she agitated herself madly on me in a hurricane of wild heavings and wrigglings and squirmings, in which I joined with frenzied up-thrusting—till, no longer able to refrain, I shot a torrent of boiling love juice into Helen just as she, for the third time, yielded to nature and spent in exquisite transports of rapture! Oh God!, how I spent into her—and how ecstatically Helen received the deluge of hot semen that I poured frantically into her! Then we both collapsed and lay motionless, clinging rapturously to each other!

How long we thus lay I do not know! I came to first. Helen was lying on me limp and nerveless, her head resting on my shoulder—she had fainted under the violence of her spending and the intensity of her spasm of pleasure! Gently and caressingly I passed my hands over her naked self, squeezing her breasts and endeavouring to bring her to herself, all the while whispering fond words of love in her ear! Presently Helen moved uneasily, then drew a long breath, or rather a deep sigh, of utter satisfaction and slowly raised her head half-consciously with a glazed look. As her humid eyes opened they met mine and flashed instant recognition. A wonderful smile indicative of the intense satisfaction and happiness radiated her face— "Jack! My darling!" she murmured rapturously, as she pressed her lips to mine and showered kisses on me till we both gasped for breath! Then slowly and reluctantly she drew herself off my now limp and dejected prick, rose, and tottered to her bathroom. Promptly I slipped into my room and indulged in a welcome and necessary ablution, then returned to Helen's room just as she herself re-appeared. She ran straight into my welcoming arms. I led her to a chair and installed her on my knees, and in soft murmurs and with loving kisses we testified to each other the pleasure we had mutually tasted!

"Now my darling, good night!" I said finally and drew Helen tenderly to me!

"Goddd night, my darling, darling Jack!" she murmured as our lips sought each other—"Oh! how happy you have made me!" and passionately she kissed me, then rose and led me to my door, as she had to lock it after me.

"Sleep well, my darling!" she added archly— "Do not forget that tomorrow night you have to violate Alice!" I laughed, gave her a final kiss and thus we parted!

And so ended our first evening at *The Nunnery*!

CHAPTER FOUR

We all met at breakfast next morning, the ladies looking radiant; Helen and Maud's faces wore a look of happy satisfaction, while Alice was a veritable blush-rose! After the usual bright meal, Helen disappeared into her boudoir to write letters, and Maud adjourned to her bedroom for mysteries in millinery connected with a visit she was about to pay. Alice confessed to having no plans; to me she seemed nervous and pre-occupied, her thoughts no doubt reverting constantly to her ordeal of the evening. Since I arrived and had been told of the wonderful and almost incredible thing she was willing to do, I was most anxious to get her by herself for a little so that I might let her understand how I appreciated it—but no opportunity had been vouchsafed; and so I decided to monopolize her all the morning, for I felt morally certain that she then would be all the happier when she was made over to me that evening in Helen's room,—and to that end I suggested that I should take her on the river till lunch time. Delightedly she accepted the proposition, and soon we were in the boat and off, she in the stern seats with the tiller ropes, and I on the rowing thwart, in easy chatting distance of her.

She had on a walking dress—and what between the lowness of her seat and the shortness of her dress, more of her shapely legs and slender ankles cased in dainty stockings were visible to my delighted eyes than she quite approved of; and she strove by sundry tugs and re-adjustments to lessen the exhibition—but without success. I watched her in amused silence—and when she resigned herself to the inevitable and resumed her usual pose on the stern cushions with slightly heightened colour, conscious that my eyes were admiringly dwelling on her pretty extremities, I frankly laughed out and said chaffingly, "Well, you are a funny girl, Alice—why are you so unkind this morning in the matter of showing yourself to me, when you were so sweet and kind last night, and are going to be so again to-night!"

Alice coloured deeply, then laughed in pretty confusion and said, "Places and surroundings have to be considered, Jack my dear,—I am quite sure

74

that you would not like me here now just as I was last night!"

"Wouldn't I!" I rejoined ardently,—"When we get to that little sheltered backwater on the left, I'll row in, so as to give you an opportunity of changing your attire!"

"You're very considerate—and I'm much obliged to you, Jack," she replied, laughing merrily and apparently quite at her ease with me—" but I'm afraid you must deny yourself the ... may I say, pleasure!" she added archly.

"Well, I suppose lovely woman must have her way! At all events, we'll go in all the same," I replied with mock resignation—"Steer in, dear, and take us right to the end in the thick of the trees,"—and soon we found ourselves in a delicious nook and in absolute privacy. I tied the boat to a convenient root so that we could not drift, then I squeezed myself into the stern seats by Alice's side (she sweetly making room for me) and slipped my left arm round her waist.

"This is very romantic!" I remarked softly as I drew her to me—"Will not the poetry of the spot tempt you to become a wood nymph?"

Alice laughed gaily and shook her head. "I never went in for theatricals, Jack," she rejoined.

"I'm not asking you to do so now, dear," I replied—"Theatrics mean dressing up, my suggestion implied the very contrary!"

She laughed merrily, then nestling close to me

she whispered gently, blushing divinely "In less than twelve hours you'll see what you wish, Jack won't that do, dear?"

I clasped her tightly to me and made her shift herself onto my lap, then I kissed her passionately. "My darling!" I whispered, "I was only teasing you! ... And are you really going to be so sweet and kind to me to-night as to give me your ... maiden self!"

Alice smiled tenderly and gently nodded her hear, her eyes looking lovingly into mine. I kissed her sweetly and gratefully and for a moment or two our emotions enforced silence.

Presently I whispered "Tell me, darling, do you really wish this? Are you really willing to ... lose your virginity, your maidenhead?"

A vivid blush suffused her cheeks—for a few moments she was silent and I could feel how she was trembling; then she murmured with deep emotion "Had anyone else ... been suggested, I would have said indignantly No! ... No! ... No! ... — but to you, Jack, I say Yes! ... Yes! ... Yes! ..."

I was too moved to speak! ... I could only kiss her sweet lips over and over again,—and she could read in my eyes my emotion! Helen's chaffing remark that no one but myself would ever win Alice flashed through my brain—and an overwhelming desire to reward in the one and only right way Alice's love and trust as evidenced by the wonderful sacrifice of her virginity that she was willing to make, surged through me!

I held her to me more closely than ever, and looking straight into her loving eyes I said softly "Darling, you rebuke me! You are willing to surrender to a girl's most precious treasure, and to give it to me freely and without regard to your future happiness! Will you let me do what I can to ensure that happiness to you? Alice, my darling, will you become my wife?"

She gazed at me in absolute wonder, her eyes widely open in startled surprise; it was clear that she could not believe her ears! I smiled tenderly at her and whispered, "Would you like to hear it again? Alice darling, will you become my dear little wife?"

The look of startled surprise vanished,—in its place came a simply wonderful smile,—she caught her breath,—her eyes filled with happy tears which, however, could not put out the lovelight that was in them,—her lips parted, and she murmured brokenly "Oh! Jack! . . . Jack!" as she clung lovingly to me!

I bent down and kissed her tenderly on her quivering lips, and said gently, "That means Yes! . . . Oh! My darling! . . . my darling!" And for a while we remained silent, our eyes looking into each other's and brimming over with love!

Presently Alice whispered with a curious smile,

half anxious and half roguish, "Jack! what about to-night, darling?"

I laughed, she also after a moment's hesitation. "We had better let the arrangement stand good, darling," I replied, "We must think of Helen and Maud, for were it not for them we should not now be ... sweethearts!" (she kissed me delightedly) "We must not disappoint them. I don't think we will tell them anything until after ... after." Alice blushed vividly and kissed me sweetly, "After you have tasted Love's raptured in my arms! You're happier now about it, eh darling?"

"I'm yours now entirely and absolutely, Jack," Alice murmured gently, her eyes full of love—"I'm your happy sweetheart now!—I'll gladly be your mistress to-night, and your little wife as soon as ever you like! So do just what you like with me and to me!" and she smiled lovingly and trustfully.

I kissed her gratefully, and a sweet idea came into my brain; with a mischievous smile I said "I'm going to take you at your word, darling!"— and slipped my right hand under her clothes, arresting its movement upwards when it got to her dainty knees. "Oh Jack!" she exclaimed as she started up hurriedly and strove to defend herself, at the same time laughing merrily at her discomfiture and the way I had turned her words against herself. I looked smilingly at her but kept my hand where it was on her knees. "What do you wish to do, darling?" she whispered in pretty confusion. "I want to call on a maiden that has just become engaged, and to offer her my congratulations," I replied with mock gravity—"I know she is at home and so with your leave I'll go on." Alice laughed merrily and gently reparted her thighs as my hand passed along them, as if to facilitate its approach to her cunt, all the while looking at me with eyes full of love. Delightedly, my hand travelled over her luscious thighs clad in dainty drawers, till it reached the tender junction,—then slipping through the opening it arrived at its destination. "Oh darling!" breathed Alice, squirming deliciously as she felt my fingers on her maiden cunt,—and as I pulled and played with her silky hairs and stroked and caressed her exquisitely springy and juicy flesh, she threw her arms 'round my neck and pressing her lips on mine she kissed me passionately, agitating herself charmingly all the time. Soon my finger gently made its way between the lips of her cunt and into the warm throbbing moist interior, where it inquisitively explored its sweet recesses, dwelling significantly on the weblike hymeneal membrane that I was that same evening to break through, and then as she was now beginning to wriggle in earnest I challenged her excited clitoris and set to work to frig Alice! "Oh Jack! . . . darling!" she panted rapturously as she jogged herself to meet my finger, gently at first and then more and more wildly and rapidly till in a storm of uncontrollable jerks and squirmings and wriggles the ecstatic crisis overtook her and she inundated my happy finger with her virginal love-juice!

Alice had kept her lips pressed on mine throughout, deliciously punctuating with ardent kisses her transports while being felt and frigged! When the last spasms of pleasure had died away she gave me one long clinging burning kiss and looking gratefully at me with her still humid eyes she murmured rapturously, "Oh Jack! it was just heavenly!" "Nicer than last night, dear?" I asked quizzingly. "Oh! yes, yes!" she replied in tones of the deepest conviction that set me off in a laugh in which she soon joined. "Last night I was too timid and nervous, and so awfully surprised by everything I saw, and so excited also, that I could not let myself go as I did just now!" she added colouring prettily. "Then you'll let yourself go to-night, darling!" I whispered significantly. She blushed like a peony, looked tenderly at me, and with a loving smile she nodded her head assuringly!

"Now it is time for us to start home,—one final kiss, darling! I said feelingly. "We're going to be very happy, love, for we are wise enough to recognise that a bedroom has joys as well as a drawing room! Now, my sweet . . .!" and lovingly we kissed each other. Then we resumed our proper places in the boat and soon were out in the river again, this time homeward bound, talking sweet nothings in supreme happiness.

Presently, Alice, with a little hesitation, said somewhat seriously, "Please promise me one thing, Jack!—When we are married please keep on being kind and good to Auntie Helen and to Maud!—I shall be so very miserable if I should be the cause of their being left without the sexual satisfaction they so ardently desire and need! You will promise this, Jack darling?"

I was very touched by her devotion. "I promise willingly, dear," I replied earnestly—then with a mischievous smile I added, "We'll have our bedrooms arranged like those in the Nunnery, darling. We will always put up Auntie Helen and Maud in the rooms that communicate with ours, so that they can slip in quietly—and we'll have regular orgies when they come up, eh, darling!"

Alice beamed on me, then laughed merrily, exclaiming, "Oh Jack! It will be fun!"

As we neared the house, Helen came down to meet us. "I've been wondering what became of you two!" she exclaimed,— "Now come along, lunch is ready—we must feed you up, Alice darling, and you also, Jack," she added laughingly, and, slipping her arm round Alice, she led her towards the house. I fastened the boat and tidied up generally, and then followed them.

CHAPTER FIVE

After lunch the ladies retired, frankly admitting that they were going to "rest" so as to better fit them for the excitements of the evening. I announced my intention of walking to the neighbouring little town to try and do some shopping; but they all so vigorously protested against my taking an eight mile walk and knocking myself up that at Helen's pressing request I consented to be driven in. The object of my visit was to try to obtain two pairs of strong leather wristlets, softly padded and fitted with a brass "D" so that they could be strapped together or each arm secured singly. I was fortunate enough to find the very thing at the saddler's; he stitched the "D"s on while I waited, and I bore them off in triumph. My readers will come across them presently.

I was back to The Nunnery by tea time, after which Maud took Alice off for a short walk, while Helen and I strolled in the gardens. She was delightfully full of the pleasures she had tasted in my arms on the previous night,—"Jack! I'm another woman today!" she exclaimed rapturously, adding with a merry smile "I didn't know I wanted it so badly!" She went on to tell me that she had kept Alice with her all that afternoon as she feared that the girl's natural apprehension of the ordeal of being ravished might make her nervous and perhaps hysterical when the moment arrived, were she allowed to think about it too much previously— but, she said, "While Alice does seem a little to dread the . . . operation itself, she really seems to be almost looking forward to surrendering her maidenhead to you! I'm sure she loves you, Jack!"

"Dear little thing!" I replied with feeling—"The thought of having to ravish her this evening excites me terribly!"

Half-past ten again was a very long time in coming, but at last the clock chimed the half hour, and promptly I entered Helen's room, where I found Maud and Alice, the latter really looking nervous and agitated, although she greeted me with a sweet smile. We kissed each other all round, and then Helen placed Alice in my arms with a significant smile that made the blushing girl grow still more rosy as I fondly kissed her again, and then passed my arm round her waist so as to keep her with me.

"Now let us begin!" I said briskly. "Helen, may we move that long dress box of yours with the padded top into the middle of the room?" Quickly she and Maud effected the change, then looked enquiringly at me. "Thanks, dears!" I said—"Now Helen, lie down on your back, naked, with your legs widely apart, and let me have a good study of your cunt!"

"Oh Jack!" she exclaimed, colouring vividly as she looked pleadingly at me—but I only laughed at her and pointed to the box; whereupon Helen reluctantly took off her nightie and placed herself on her back in the position desired. Quickly I knelt between her knees with Maud and Alice on either side of me, their eyes gleaming with excitement, and together we delightedly inspected Helen's superb cunt—gazing admiring on the thickly clustering growth of hairs of Venus' Hill and the delicate salmon-pink of its lips, poor Helen all the while blushing like a schoolgirl! Then with gentle fingers I drew the lips apart and disclosed Helen's clitoris (evidently much excited), the quivering folds of pink tender flesh, and the delicious passage in which I had already been twice voluptuously lodged!

At last I removed my hands, and leaning forward I ardently kissed Helen on her cunt, she squirming prettily,—and rose. "Don't move yet dear," I said, —"Now Maud, strip yourself naked and lie on your Mother face upwards—let your legs hand down outside hers, so that we can compare both cunts!"

"Oh Jack!" both Mother and daughter cried aghast as they looked ashamedly at each other; but I was obdurate. Alice was now rosy red, but her eyes glittered with eager anticipation, and she smiled delightedly at me as our eyes met; she undoubtedly was enjoying herself!

Reluctantly Maud complied. When she had stripped herself naked I made her straddle across Helen, then gently lowered her backwards till she lay flat on her Mother, who passed her arms round her daughter and maintained her in the desired position! Their cunts now were displayed one just above the other, a charming spectacle!

"Now Alice dear, strip yourself naked also!" I said gently to her. Much surprised and somewhat disconcerted, Alice slowly complied, and shame-facedly stood naked before me; after a delightful but hasty glance at her lovely timid shrinking naked figure I made her kneel between Helen's parted legs and sit on her heels, then I myself knelt behind her, passed my arms round her and gently seized her breasts—my chin resting on her right shoulder, so that we could together feast our eyes on the piquant sight, the cunts of mother and daughter!

In admiring silence we gazed our fill, Alice's trembles testifying to her suppressed excitement: "Aren't they sweet!" I whispered. Alice nodded eagerly, too excited to speak, her eyes shining with something akin to lust! After a little further silent contemplation I whispered again "Open Maud's cunt, dear, so that we can see what the inside is like!" Joyously Alice complied, and with her pretty little fingers she pulled widely apart the delicate lips of Maud's cunt and revealed the lovely interior, salmon-tinted and juicy, surmounted by a projecting and angry-looking clitoris, which seemed to attract Alice's eyes.

"Now open Auntie Helen's dear;" I whispered. Quickly Alice lowered her hands, and placing the tips of her fingers on either side of Helen's well-defined and pouting slit she held Helen's cunt open for my inspection! "Do you see any family likeness, dear?" I asked with a smile.

Alice laughed silently—"Of course!" she said softly, "They're exactly like each other, only Auntie's is so much bigger and ... and ... looser!" she added with a mischievous smile which made me fondle and squeeze her dear little breasts more actively than before! Then of her own accord Alice began to stroke and play with the glorious pair of cunts in front of her, devoting a hand to each— while Helen and Maud wriggled and squirmed deliciously, uttering involuntarily little cries of pleasure as Alice's gentle fingers wandered caressingly over their sensitive and ticklish cunts—her eyes dancing with delight!

"I think they have had enough, dear!" I said presently and Alice and I rose and assisted Helen and Maud to their feet.

"Now Jack, Alice must let us examine her virgin cunt before you alter it forever!" cried Maud excitedly.

"Oh no, Maud! Oh no, Jack, please!" Alice pleaded, blushing vividly.

"I'd also like to study it, dear?" I said, "and this will be our last chance. So lie down, darling!"

Shamefacedly and with burning blushes Alice showly complied; delightedly Helen and Maud forced her legs widely apart and, kneeling together between them, they proceeded to examine Alice's maiden treasure, while behind them I also knelt, my head between theirs, my arms round them both, my hands each occupied with a breast of each. After minutely inspecting Alice's full and prominent *Mons Veneris* and gently playing with the hair that grew so prettily on it, they tenderly pulled the delicate close-fitting lips apart and excitedly gazed at the virgin interior, the web-like membrane that defended the stronghold of Alice's virginity receiving their closest and most interested attention. "There's your job, Jack!" exclaimed Maud wickedly, as she pointed to it—on hearing which, poor Alice shivered involuntarily but most prettily.

At last they rose. "Darling! it's very sweet!" murmured Helen in Alice's ear as she fondly kissed her and began to help her to rise. Meanwhile, I had attracted Maud's attention, and protruding the tip of my tongue between my lips I made her understand my intentions. She nodded delightedly and quickly got behind Alice and caught hold of her breasts and so prevented her from getting up, while I said gently, "Lie still, dear, we want you a little longer!" and knelt down on her right motioning to Helen to place herself similarly on Alice's left.

"Oh! Jack! what are you going to do to me?" Alice cried, half alarmed by these mysterious preparations. "Something very sweet, darling!" cried Maud,—"Don't be frightened, just lie still!" In an undertone, I directed Helen to hold Alice's left leg firmly while I imprisoned her right leg between my right arm and my side,—then bending down, I placed my lips on Alice's tender cunt and lovingly kissed it!!

In spite of Maud's re-assuring words, Alice had been watching my every movement intently; she saw my head bend forward and down—then she felt my lips touch her cunt and imprint on it a kiss that sent a quiver through her. Startled by the sensations now aroused she cried, "Oh Jack! don't," and tried to close her legs and rise—but we were too strong for her and forced her to remain as she was. Again I kissed her sweet cunt,—again she quivered violently and struggled to get free, crying

"Don't Jack! Please don't!" Her face was now like a peony and she was thrilling every limb—my kisses on her maiden cunt had evidently set her on fire and her lustful desires had passed beyond her control. Just then I imprinted a burning kiss on her clitoris itself, pressing my lips down on her soft springing flesh as I did so.

"Ah!" Alice ejaculated sharply, agitating herself divinely as her lust began to dominate her. Then I lightly ran the tip of my tongue along her tender slit, and began to lick the lips of her cunt!

"Oh! ... oh! ..." Alice gasped in a strange half-strangled voice, closing her eyes in ecstasy,—no longer resisting but yielding to her now imperious erotic desires! Helen to whom this sweet pastime was an absolutely new revelation, was a study—with eager gleaming eyes, dilated nostrils, and slightly parted lips watched Alice with the keenest interest, Alice now being in the throes of the wildest erotic frenzy, wriggling, quivering deliciously, thrilling with rapture as my loving tongue tickled and licked her now inflamed cunt! I ceased for a moment to feast my eyes on her and to exchange significant smiles with Maud and Helen—then I whispered to the latter "Help me to hold Alice's cunt open so that I can get my tongue inside!" at the same time placing my left hand alongside of Alice's slit. Quickly comprehending my wishes Helen placed her fingers opposite to mine, and together we pulled Alice's cunt widely open,—then after an admiring glance at its pinky juicy luscious interior now evidently throbbing in intense sexual excitement I inserted my tongue deeply into it and began to agitate it subtly with uncontrollable desire! Wildly she tossed and jerked herself upwards as if to meet the thrusts of my tongue, her head rolling from side to side in her blissful transports and her breasts dancing with the palpitations of her heaving bosom, while she ejaculated brokenly incoherent exclamations in the fury of her erotic rage! I saw it was time to bring on the ecstatic crisis, and so my tongue attacked her throbbing and excited clitoris, sucking and tickling it passionately! "Ha! ... ha! ... ha! ...", she cried chokingly in a paroxysm of rapture, then she spent frantically in exquisite bliss and delicious spasmodic quivering as my still devoted tongue absorbed the sweet maiden love-juice of her hot discharge as it revelled in its delicious environment between the lips of her cunt!

When I found that the spasms of pleasure were ceasing to thrill through Alice, I withdrew my tongue and lips from her cunt and rose. As I did so, Helen gave a gasp of astonishment and pointed to my mouth with an expression of horror, for my moustache was plentifully bedewed with Alice's spendings. I chuckled contentedly at her and disappeared into my room where I quickly put myself in order again and then rejoined her. Alice had just come to herself,—Helen and Maud were kneeling on each side of her and kissing her fondly as they stroked her breasts as if to stimulate her. I heard Maud say softly "Didn't I tell you, dear, that you were going to taste something very delicious?—Oh! you are a lucky girl!"

Just then Alice caught sight of me—she sprang up, threw herself into my erms, flung hers round my neck and kissed me passionately over and over again, murmuring, "Oh darling! ... Darling!" till she had to cease for want of breath. Then Maud took her off for a necessary toilet, leaving me with Helen.

By now I was in a furious state of erection—it was absolutely necessary to me to get some relief from somebody. I seized Helen and whispered fiercely "Will Alice be ready to be ravished when she comes back or must she be allowed to wait a bit?"

"Better let her wait a little, dear," she answered looking sympathisingly at me—and I could see that she also was very erotically excited and was longing for relief!

"Then either you or Maud will have to take me on, dear!" I replied, "I must have one of you,— feel," and I conducted her hand to my raging prick!

"Oh, Poor thing!" she exclaimed, adding with a smile, "Either Maud or I will e delighted to have it inserted into us, dear. Who shall it be?"

"You, darling, if I dare choose!" I answered,

"but we had better get Alice to deal the cards and settle that way. Here she comes!" and as I spoke, Alice and Maud appeared, Alice absolutely radiant with delight.

I tore off my night kit and pointed to my prick in tremendous erection. "Alice darling, please deal the cards to Helen and Maud and settle who is to have the honour—whoever gets the Ace of Spades must be the one to relieve me!"

Excitedly, Alice shuffled and cut the cards, then dealt them face upwards to Maud and Helen; after a few rounds the Ace of Spades fell before Helen. A look of delight flashed over her face as she looked delightedly at me.

"Come, darling!" I said. She wanted no pressing, but quickly slipped on the bed and placed herself in position. In a moment I was on her—in another I had buried my prick in her expectant cunt. Then, clasping her tightly against me, I rammed fiercely into her—she ably seconded my furious movements, and soon we both spent ecstatically, she quivering rapturously as she felt herself inundated by my boiling discharge! A rapid but most delicious fuck!

"Quick Jack! Let me up!" Helen whispered. Hastily, but reluctantly, I rose off her and set her free, laughing as she rushed off to her bathroom followed by Maud.

"May I come with you, Jack?" whispered Alice timidly. "Yes, of course, dear, come along!" I replied, looking fondly at her, then slipping my arm round her waist, I led into my room and put the door to. "Oh Jack! do let me do you, dear!" she asked excitedly, her eyes beaming merrily,—and without waiting for a reply she set to work, and in the sweetest and most delicious fashion she sponged and bathed my prick, the touch of her gentle little hands thrilling through me and reviving me wonderfully.

When she had finished I took her little hands in mine and thanked her with a kiss—then said softly, "Now dear, in about quarter of an hour I propose to take you and ... violate you sweetly! May I do so?"

Alice looked straight in the eyes lovingly and trustfully, then replied gently "Yes, darling!" then held up her lips to be kissed. "You are quite sure, sweetheart?" I asked searchingly, but with a tender smile. "Quite sure, Jack!" she replied, blushing prettily as she again met my eyes squarely and bravely, "Take me, and ... fuck me, darling!" she whispered and hid her face on my shoulder in bashful confusion. I clasped her closely against me and sought her lips with mine, and kissed her passionately over and over again till she gasped for breath.

"Now let us go back," I said, and we returned together to Helen's room which we found empty. "Oh! I'm so glad we're first back," Alice exclaimed delightedly—"They won't know that I've been with you!—Jack. Don't tell them, dear!" she added merrily, smiling her thanks as I gave the required promise. Just then Helen and Maud appeared. Helen ran up to me, threw herself into my arms and kissed me, saying laughingly, "Jack dear, it was just heavenly!"

"Darling, of course it was," I replied, "For you fuck like an angel!"—at which interchange of compliments Alice and Maud laughed heartily, Helen soon joining them.

"Come to me, Alice dear," said Helen as she seated herself in her favorite chair, "You and I are entitled to a rest!"—and quickly Alice settled herself in Helen's lap and, greatly daring, gently played with her Auntie's breasts.

"I suppose that means that you and I are not entitled at present to rest, eh dear?" I said to Maud meaningly,—"Come and discuss the situation!" and seating myself I drew her on my knees and gently toyed with her cunt.

"Well Jack," she said presently, "What are we to do?"

"I'm afraid your choice is limited to finger or tongue, dear," I replied with a significant smile.

"And a very sweet option too!" Maud answered cheerily,—"Jack, I'd like to be sucked, a long slow suck!" And she looked at me invitingly. We rose, and I arranged her on Helen's box, face upwards, with her legs nicely apart, Helen and Alice kneeling one on each side of her the better to watch the proceedings, Alice being particularly keen to witness what she herself had just tasted so deliciously.

After a little sweet toying with Maud's cunt, I stooped down and kissed it ardently, my lips travelling right along the coral slit and making Maud quiver voluptuously—while Helen and Alice intuitively commenced to play with her breasts. Then I ran my tongue slowly along the lovely opening, touching it very lightly, and evidently giving Maud exquisite pleasure—for she began to wriggle delightfully, half jogging herself up as if to meet my tongue, whereupon I stiffened it and forced the tip well into her orifice, then stabbed and darted and thrust downwards strongly, first slowly and then more rapidly as I noticed her agitation increase. Again I ran my tongue along her slit, this time with more of a licking action, reverting to the orifice every now and then—till I had worked her up to a frenzy of unsatisfied longing lust without touching her clitoris. Maud's movements now became tumultuous, even lascivious, and wanton in their wrigglings and writhings, their twistings and contortions; she was evidently on the point of spending and longing to spend, but yet delaying the culmination of her pleasure in order to prolong the blissful agony of the struggle against herself! Being desirous of humouring her desires I continued my alternate lickings and thrustings, avoiding touching her clitoris—but soon it was patent to me that Maud was losing her powers of self-control.

Promptly I attacked her clitoris, sometimes simply licking and tickling it, sometimes taking it gently between my lips and sucking it! Maud now seemed to go mad! Alice told me afterwards that she was an extraordinary sight in her erotic fury! She plunged, curvetted, wriggled, and tossed herself about so wildly that I had the greatest difficulty in keeping my mouth planted on her cunt! Suddenly her body stiffened, her breasts became tense, an indescribable spasm convulsed her —and with a delirously strangled, "Ah ... h!" she spent rapturously, her whole body thrilling voluptuously as the spasms of pleasure quivered through her, while she distilled her love juice so plentifully that my tongue lips and moustache all were spattered with her feminine essence of love!

Again Helen's shocked eyes met mine as I raised my head from her daughter's cunt, and again I chuckled contentedly at her as I went off to my room, leaving Maud in her charge till she came to! I was more than jubilant—I had now done my duty to both Helen and Maud, and now I was about to enjoy the exquisite pleasure of depriving Alice of her virginity!

I hurried back as quickly as I could. Maud had recovered and had got up, and was on her way to the bathroom when I appeared. She stopped, threw her arms round me fondly and kissed me passionately over and over again,—then said roguishly, "Jack, your tongue is really almost as good as you

... prick!" then vanished, followed by Alice and our merry laughter.

"Now I suppose you will take Alice, Jack!" said Helen eagerly. I nodded. "Then I'll get everything ready for her!" she rejoined, with a meaning smile as she produced the towels she had provided to protect her bed quilt from the tell-tale stains that Alice's defloration was sure to cause. She glanced at my prick. "You are hardly ready yet, Jack!— We'll have to work you up, Sir!" she added smilingly. "Let me make a start," and seating me at her side she commenced to play with my limp and flaccid penis. The touch of her hand was heavenly, and soon I began to feel my forces revive.

Maud and Alice now re-appeared, and when the latter caught sight of the bed so obviously prepared for her and saw Helen getting me ready, her courage seemed suddenly to leave her; she nervously exclaimed, "Oh! I can't! ... I can't do it!" and tried to run away into her room! But Maud caught her and held her gently but firmly, and said with an encouraging smile "Nonsense dear! Here Mother, will you take Alice and give me Jack, and I'll have him ready in two twos in a way that you do not know! Come along, Jack!" I guessed her intention and laughed, then made way for Alice—who was quickly folded in Helen's arms and soon soothed and caressed till she had recovered from her sudden timidity. I think, however, that the sight of Maud and me had more to do with her reviving interest.

Maud had made me lie on my back on Helen's dress box—with a gentle thumb and forefinger she had raised my limp prick and with the other hand she had gently captured my balls—and she was just beginning to sweetly lick the latter and tickle the former with her kind tongue, to the unbounded astonishment of both Helen and Alice, the latter evidently forgetting her nervousness in the excitement caused by Maud's proceedings! "See, mother," exclaimed Maud presently, "Jack is coming along finely!—I'll have him ready for you, Alice, in a minute!" and with eyes dancing with delight, she resumed her delicious ministrations and soon my prick was standing stiff and rampant and ready to ravish Alice!

"Come dear!" said Helen to Alice as soon as she saw I was ready; then she and Maud let the still reluctant and nervous girl to the bed, and having made her lie down, they drew her legs apart and generally arranged her to receive me. Then each kissed her tenderly, whispering something that I did not catch, but which brought the blushes again to Alice's cheeks. "Now, Jack!" said Helen invitingly, "She's ready for you!" and she pointed to Alice's maiden cunt lying so deliciously and temptingly open to attack.

I hurried to the bed, stooped over Alice, and whispered, "Give me your last maiden kiss, darling! and fairly sucked the life out of her mouth, then quickly I slipped on to the bed, got between

Alice's legs, and lowering myself gently on to her I brought the head of my prick to bear on her little cunt—then shoving firmly, but gently, I succeeded in getting it into her a little way, then my progress was blocked!

Tightening my clasp of her, I shoved harder and harder, but without breaking through her maiden defences, and evidently hurting her, for she cried "Oh Jack!", as if in pain, at the same time wriggling uncomfortably and apprehensively! Collecting myself, I lunged strongly downwards—something seemed to give way, and my prick seemed to glide into a sheath of delicious warmth and exquisite softness, while a smothered shriek from Alice proclaimed to Helen and Maud that she had lost her maidenhead! Taking every care not to hurt her needlessly, I drove my prick deeper and deeper up her virgin sheath till I was fully buried in her, our hairs intermingling, then my mouth sought hers, and passionately I kissed her quivering lips, receiving from her her first kiss as a woman!

Oh! my sensations of triumph! I was possessing Alice, I had captured her maidenhead, and she was now lying quivering and trembling, closely locked in my arms with my prick buried in her—and now I was about to give her the sweetest of lessons! Delightedly I set to work to fuck her in earnest, going slowly and gently at first for I was afraid of hurting her—but when I noted that her nervousness and pain were turning deliciously to wondering rapture and heavenly ecstasy as I agitated myself on her, holding her tightly clasped against me, I began to move more and more freely. Soon Alice herself began to respond—I could feel her bosom commencing to heave and palpitate, her breathing became broken and agitated, and then she commenced to move herself under me in the most deliciously provocative manner, which fairly set me going. Quicker and quicker I rammed into her—wilder and more tumultuous became our movements! Then came the climax, and deliriously I spent into Alice, deluging her virgin interior with my boiling tribute which she received with wondering rapture and indescribable bliss while she simultaneously surrendered herself to the dictates of her newly-born lust and spent in the most exquisite transports of delight!

We lay locked tightly in each other's arms, motionless save for the involuntary quivers occasioned by lingering spasms of pleasure. Gladly would I have continued to remain so, but Helen begged me to get off Alice so as to set her free to be carried off to the bathroom and looked after! And after imprinting a passionate kiss on her unconscious lips I reluctantly rose and hurried off to my room.

When I returned I found Maud waiting for me. In reply to my eager enquiries she told me with an assuring smile that Alice was "quite all right and very happy now that the ordeal had been passed"

—that I had hurt her very little indeed, but not unnaturally her cunt was sore and should be left for the present untouched till tomorrow evening when I would find Alice only too ready to be fucked again.

While we were talking, Helen and Alice returned. I took Alice in my arms and after some tender kisses I told Helen and Maud of our arrangements for the future and (at Alice's request) of her wish that we all should continue to live as we then were doing and enjoy each other all round. Their surprise and delight I will not attempt to describe. Suffice it to say that after mutual congratulations and compliments, Helen insisted on the seance being closed, so that we all might get the benefit of a long night's rest so as to enjoy the following evening thoroughly—for, as she said with an arch smile, "We women will all be equal and ready for anything and everything whenever wanted!" And then after tender good-nights all round we retired to our respective rooms.

CHAPTER SIX

At breakfast next morning I was delighted to see all three ladies appear as radiant as ever, Alice especially. She was looking more charming and attractive than I had ever seen her; her nervo-erotic excitement had been sweetly allayed, she had now no ordeal to dread, and she had the proud satisfaction of feeling that she now stood level with Maud and Helen in matters sexual, and could do whatever they did—and this combination of happy circumstances made her eyes sparkle and imparted to her a pretty vivacity that was simply bewitching and made me look forward to enjoying her in the coming evening. There was no doubt that all three had been badly in need of sexual satisfaction and were revelling in the pleasures they had tasted naked in my arms and I doubt whether a happier trio could have been found in the country.

But the morning post brought a danger in the form of a letter to Maud from the friends she was looking forward to visit. It begged her to come to them at once—not later at all events than the following day—so that she might join in sundry frivolities that had been hastily organized.

"I must go!" she wailed half-mournfully—"For I haven't any excuse except that I want to stay here and be fucked by Jack, and I can't possibly give that as a reason for not going!" she added with a quizzical smile; "Oh! isn't it unfortunate!" she exclaimed.

"Cheer up, dear!" I cried as I laughed at her really comical despair—"Don't forget that I now have to make week ends to see my sweetheart, who says that you and Helen may borrow me! So it is not as bad as it might be!"

Maud brightened up at once. "Thanks for reminding me, Jack!" she answered smilingly—then turning to Alice she said "And thanks to you darling, for as kind and unselfish a thing as ever one girl did for another!" and going over to Alice she kissed her gratefully and lovingly. "Jack!" she exclaimed, "you must plan a regular orgie for tonight, one that will keep me going for a week!" and she laughed happily.

"All right!" I replied, joining in her gaiety,— "Let us adjourn to the garden out of earshot, and see what brilliant ideas we can raise!" and we all trooped off merrily and settled ourselves under the trees, and set to work to think hard.

I broke the silence after a little time by asking, "Has anyone anything to suggest?" They all nodded negatively with a conscious laugh. "Then let me put my idea before you, such as it is!" I added, smiling at the eagerness with which they all leant forward to listen, their eyes fixed expectantly on me.

I proceeded. "When I was in Budapest I saw a game played by three girls and a man; its name translated into English was "The Victim and her Torturers." One of the girls was chosen by lot to be the Victim, the others then became the Torturers, the man being the Chief Torturer and the others were to obey him implicitly. All four stripped themselves naked—the Victim was then tied down securely on a bed, and for a certain specified time the others did just what they liked to her, their object being to make her spend as often as possible by teasing and provoking and exciting her, no pain-causing play being allowed. Every now and then some two of the Torturers seemed to find the game too exciting—then they would mutually satisfy each others lustful desires while the third looked on and let the Victim have a bit of rest in which to pull herself together a little.

"How would this game suit us for tonight? We are three women and one man. As Maud wants as much as she can get tonight, we might make her Victim and give her a good hour's doing—during which we Torturers can also enjoy ourselves as our natures may demand! Or I shall be Victim. The Victim, I ought to have explained is considered to have the best of the fun. Or each of you can have a twenty minutes turn, drawing cards to settle the order!

Helen, Maud, and Alice looked interrogatively at each other, then broke into hearty laughter. "A most excellent idea, Jack dear!" exclaimed Helen, —"what do you say, girls?" Maud and Alice nodded delightedly. "Carried unanimously!" declared Helen, adding with an affectionate glance at me "With our best thanks to Jack!"

"Now I had better leave you to settle among yourselves which of the three alternatives is to be the order of the evening—I'd rather that you decided this without me. So I'll stroll to the river and back," and I rose.

"One moment, Jack!" cried Alice excitedly, "We want to know if the Victim will be ... fucked!" she asked with pretty blushes. We all laughed merrily. "The girl I saw as Victim was fucked twice, dear, in the hour—once by the Chief Torturer and once by me,—they saw how the game excited me and they kindly made me free of the girl! It was a piquant sensation to fuck a tied-down girl and she seemed to approve of it also!"

"Ah!" Alice exclaimed, her eyes sparkling. Then

I moved off, and they fell to work eagerly to discuss and arrange the evening's programme.

In a remarkably short time, I heard them calling me and I rejoined them. "We've settled everything, Jack!" said Helen—"We'll each have a twenty minutes turn: Maud first, Alice next and I last; you're to be Chief Torturer and boss of the show and we others will do as you may direct."

"Capital!" I exclaimed laughingly, "We'll have a great time!" whereon they all burst into hearty laughter.

"Now Mother, come along and help me to pack!" cried Maud as she hooked her arm into Helen's—"Alice, we leave Jack in your charge!" and off they went to the house, laughing merrily.

"What shall we do dear?" I asked of Alice, "Another row?"

"Oh yes, please, Jack!" she exclaimed delightedly, and soon we were off in the boat, she steering and I rowing. As we neared the backwater, I began to wonder whether she would take us in—and sure enough with a conscious smile she steered the boat in. I made fast as on the previous morning and then seated myself by her on the stern cushions.

"Why have you brought us in here, dear?" I asked softly as I slipped my left arm round her waist and drew her to me.

She yielded herself sweetly to my pressure, then whispered with a blush, "To thank you, darling, for what you did so sweetly to me last night!" And with love in her eyes she kissed me tenderly.

"But it is I who should thank you, Alice dear!" I replied softly, "For you let me take from you forever your most precious possession, your maidenhead!

Alice shook her head and looked tenderly at me. "If you only knew how bad I've often felt dear, and how wonderful I'm feeling now, you would understand my gratitude!"

I kissed her lovingly. "Let it be so, dear!" I replied softly, and let me show you tonight how I appreciate the privilege of fucking you!" She blushed and laughed merrily.

"Did I hurt you much, darling?" I whispered.

"Very little,—you were so gentle with me, Jack!" she said softly—"I am a little sore—but I don't intend to let it rob me of tonight's pleassures!" and she laughed gaily.

"May I judge for myself?" I whispered mischievously. Alice blushed and nodded, and slightly shifted herself so as to facilitate the movements of my eager hand which already had found its way under her clothes and was travelling along between her thighs. Soon it passed through the opening of her drawers and reached her cunt, she flinching deliciously as she felt my finger touch her cunt gently and caressingly.

"It is a bit swollen, dear," I whispered as I tenderly played with her hairs. Alice nodded, smiling happily and evidently enjoying having her cunt felt by me. After a little more toying with her hairs and her delicious flesh I gently forced my finger into her down to where her maiden barrier used to be; she winced in spite of herself as my finger touched the sore spot, but to my delight she allowed me to gently soothe the inflamed flesh, whispering "Oh Jack, that's nice!" as my finger entered the sheath-like passage now open for life, and penetrated deeper and deeper into her—the feel of her moist juicy folds of flesh being exquisitely delicious!

"Don't you think that your cunt will be all the better for a little of your own lubricant, dear, your very own manufacture?" I asked with a significant smile. For a moment Alice looked puzzled, then suddenly grasped my idea, blushed prettily, then nodded delightedly with sparkling eyes. Lovingly I set to work to frig her, agitating my finger inside her cunt—at first slowly then more and more rapidly as she wriggled and quivered with pleasure, till I attacked her excited clitoris—when she spent voluptuously, inundating my finger with her sweet essense of love, which I proceeded to distribute all over her inflamed flesh to her evident satisfaction. Then withdrawing my hand I helped her to adjust her disordered clothes, and soon we were again on the river homeward bound, mutually delighted with the little episode.

On the way home Alice told me with a rogueish

smile that they all were so eager to taste the sensation of being fucked while fastened down that they unanimously adopted the twenty minutes turn suggestion. Then she exclaimed archly "Jack, tell me some special way to excite Auntie Helen and Maud when they are tied down!" I laughed, and replied "Get your cook to give you half a dozen long and finely pointed feathers, and tickle their cunts, dear!" She clapped her little hands together in delight at the idea, exclaiming with sparkling eyes "Oh Jack! how lovely! how I'll make them wriggle tonight!" evidently overlooking the fact that any specially brilliant idea of hers would be adopted by the others when her turn to be tied down came; but the anticipation of witnessing the struggles of the three ladies in turn when the feather was applied to their respective cunts was so tempting that I refrained from warning her of the probable consequences of her enterprise.

CHAPTER SEVEN

The day passed away uneventfully, and at half-past ten we all met in Helen's room, the three ladies in visible but suppressed excitement. "We won't waste time," I said briskly, "So everyone naked please!" and in a trice, I again had the pleasure of viewing their naked charms. Then I produced the wristlets and straps, the sight of which produced much laughter; and quickly under my directions Helen and Alice fastened them on Maud's wrists and ankles.

I made her lie down face upwards on her mother's bed and secured her wrists to the opposite bedposts by the straps; then to her surprise and consternation and to Alice's undisguised delight I directed Helen and Alice to pull Maud's legs widely apart and strap her ankles to the corner posts, so that she lay spread-eagled, exposing all her most secret charms to us and utterly unable to prevent us from doing what we liked to her! In silence we gloated over the provoking spectacle—then turning to Helen and Alice I said, "Now dears, Maud is at your absolute disposal for fifteen minutes—then I shall want her to myself! Now, go ahead!"

With a cry of joy Alice threw herself on Maud's prostate and helpless self and excitedly showered kisses on her lips and cheeks and eyes, then turning herself slightly she seized hold of Maud's breasts and after kissing the pretty coral nipples, she took them between her lips and sucked each breasts in turn, all the while squeezing and handling them— Maud lying helpless in shame-faced confusion, the colour coming and going on her cheeks, and a nervous smile passing over her face when her eyes met ours. I glanced at Helen—her eyes were rivetted on her daughter's naked body and glittered with a peculiar light, and as I stealthily watched her I noticed how she was shivering! It certainly was not from cold, and recollecting how she was fascinated and excited on the first evening when her daughter stood before her naked for the first time and how she from that moment seemed never tired of looking at Maud's naked beauties, I guessed that unknown to herself a lusting desire after her daughter had sprung up in her. Seeing that Alice and Maud were absorbed with each other, Alice in the hitherto untasted pleasure of playing with another girl's naked charms, Maud with the also hitherto untasted sensations of having her most private parts invaded and handled by feminine fingers, I drew Helen out of earshot and whispered to her "You look as if you want to have Maud, eh dear?" She coloured vividly and nodded vehemently with a conscious smile, too embarassed to speak. "Why don't you then?" I continued. Helen stared at me in surprise. "Get on Maud, grip her tightly, and rub your cunt against hers sweetly."

"Oh Jack, really?" Helen stammered in growing excitement, her bosom heaving with her agitation.

I nodded with a reassuring smile, adding, "Try it, dear!—Lots of women solace themselves in this way when they cannot get what they really want!" She looked incredulously at me. I smiled encouragingly; then her eyes wandered to Maud, who was lying motionless save for an occasional quiver— Alice had deserted her sweet breasts and was now busily engaged with her cunt, which she was kissing and stroking and examining, the procedure evidently giving Maud the most exquisite pleasure judging from her half-closed eyes and her beatific expression,—a most voluptuous sight, which apparently swept away Helen's hesitation. She turned to me and murmured almost inaudibly "I long to do it, Jack, but she wouldn't like it!"

I took her trembling hands, that betrayed her lust, and whispered coaxingly "Maud has got to put up with anything that any of us wish to do to her during her twenty minutes turn, dear—when she guesses what you contemplate she probably will protest, but as soon as she feels your cunt on hers she will love you more than ever! Try her, dear!" Helen hesitated, looked hungrily and longingly at Maud, and then at me, then back at Maud. At that juncture Alice exclaimed "I'm only keeping on till you come, Auntie!" Helen shivered again, her eyes now glittering wildly with lust and desire, then with an effort she muttered huskily "Jack! I must ... have her!" and moved towards the bed.

"Come along, Auntie! I've got Maud nicely excited, and you can now finish her off in any way you like!" exclaimed Alice merrily; and after imprinting a farewell kiss on Maud's cunt she rose as if to make way for Helen, while Maud languidly opened her eyes and dreamily smiled a welcome to her Mother; but when she saw Helen scramble on to the bed and place herself between her widely parted legs in an attitude that could only indicate one intention and noted the lust that was glittering in Helen's eyes she became alarmed, and cried "No, no, Mother, no, no!" as she desperately tried to break loose,—while Alice flushed as red as a peony, her colour surging right down to her breasts as she intently watched Helen with eyes widely open and startled surprise. Helen paused a moment as if gloating over the naked beauties of her daughter, then she let herself down gently on Maud who again cried "No, no, Mother, no!" as she felt her Mother's weight come on her and her Mother's arms close firmly round her as Helen arranged herself on Maud—first breast against breast, then cunt on cunt—then having her daughter at her mercy she began to move herself on her lasciviously, just as if she was lying impaled on a man!

Hardly had she commenced to agitate herself on Maud than the latter exclaimed in an indescribable tone of astonished delight, "Oh! ... oh! ... oh! ... Mummy . . dar ... ling!" which sent Alice's blushes surging again all over her bosom as she glanced shame-facedly at me. I crossed over to her and slipped my arms round her, noting as she nestled against me how she was quivering with erotic excitement! Helen had evidently set her daughter's lust on fire, for Maud now was wildly agitating and tossing herself about under her Mother and heaving herself furiously up as if to press her cunt more closely against her Mother's as she passionately kissed Helen. Suddenly she wriggled violently, then spent in delicious thrills and quiverings,—Alice's gentle but subtle toyings had so inflamed her that it needed but little to finish her! Recognizing what had happened Helen suspended her movements and rested lovingly on Maud whom she set to work to kiss ardently, evidently enjoying the thrills and spasms that convulsed her daughter as she spent. Soon Maud began to respond to her Mother's provocations and agitated herself under Helen in the most abandoned and lascivious way, which set Helen off in a fresh frenzy of uncontrollable lust. With wildly heaving buttocks and tempetuous wrigglings of her hips and bottom Helen pressed her cunt more closely than ever against her daughter's, rubbing her clitoris against Maud's till Maud again spent rapturously. Suddenly Helen's body stiffened and grew rigid—then an indescribable convulsion swept violently through her, and with incoherent ejaculations and gasps she spent madly on Maud's cunt—then collapsed and lay inert on her daughter, motionless save for the voluptuous thrills that quivered through her with each spasm of spending! And so Mother and daughter lay in a delirium of ecstasy, their cunts pressed against each other, utterly absorbed in the sensations of the moment and the divine pleasure that for the first time in their lives they had mutually given to each other!

In delighted silence Alice and I watched this voluptous episode and when the delirious climax had passed she turned to me and huskily whispered "Jack! oh Jack!" and looked pleadingly into my eyes. I saw what she wanted; I drew her closer against me and slipped my hand down to her throbbing and excited cunt. She was so madly worked up that it only required one or two quick but gentle movements of my finger to make her spend ecstati-

cally, and her thrills of rapture as she stood upright
supported by me nearly sent me off! But with a
strong effort I controlled myself, for in a minute or
two I had to fuck Maud. So I bade her run away
and freshen herself and to bring the feathers with
her when she returned; then being curious to see
how Helen and Maud would regard each other
when they came to themselves, now that their fit of
lust had been satiated, I watched them closely.

Very soon, with a long drawn breath of intense
satisfaction Maud dreamily opened her eyes—she
seemed hardly conscious; but when she found herself unable to move hand or foot and recognized
that her Mother was lying on her the happenings of
the evening instantly flashed through her brain and
sent the hot colour surging over her cheeks and
bosom at the consciousness that she had just been
ravished by her Mother; and when her eyes caught
mine she coloured more furiously than ever, but
smiled gratefully as I noiselessly clapped my hands
together with a congratulatory smile. Then she
turned her face towards her Mother and a look of
intense love came over her as she regarded her still
unconscious Mother. She brought her lips to bear
on Helen's cheek and kissed her lovingly, whispering "Mummy! ... Mummy! ... Mummy darling!
... " Then with a deep sigh Helen came to herself;
she quickly realised the position and flushed scarlet
as she half-timidly sought Maud's still humid eyes;
but when she read in them her daughter's happy

satisfaction she kissed Maud passionately and murmured in evident relief "Oh my darling! I couldn't help it! ... you looked so sweet! ... and you were so lucious!" and after another long clinging kiss she slipped off Maud.

Alice had just rejoined me, and as Helen rose to her feet our eyes inquisitively sought her cunt and that of Maud. They were a curious sight; both mother and daughter must have spent profusely as their hairs were sticky and plastered down by their joint spendings.

Noticing the direction of our looks Helen glanced at Maud's cunt and then at hers, and horrified at what she saw she exclaimed in charming confusion, "Oh Alice, do see to Maud!" and rushed off to her bathroom followed by our hearty laughter, in which Maud merrily joined with pretty blushes when we told her the cause.

Helen soon returned and joined me. "Well?" I asked mischievously. She blushed and replied softly, "Jack, it was just lovely, just wonderful!—I couldn't have believed it! Maud was simply lucious!" I laughed. "*Make* Alice do me presently, Jack!—I'd love to feel her on me!" I nodded laughingly—then glancing at the clock I exclaimed, "Only seven minutes more for Maud!—she must now be really tortured for four minutes, and then she is to be brutally outraged in your presence! Now set to work and give her a severe tickling!" and I handed a feather to each.

118

"No, no, Jack!" cried Maud, flushing painfully and tugging at her fastening—"no, no, don't tickle me! I can't stand it!"—But Helen and Alice joyously arranged themselves one on each side of her and with a smile of anticipated enjoyment they began to touch her lightly with their feathers—first in her armpits, then under her chin then all round and over her lovely breasts, Helen taking one and Alice the other—Maud all the time struggling and squirming in the most provocative way as she begged them to desist. From her breasts they passed to her navel, then on to the lines of her groin, and finally along the soft and sensitive insides of her thighs, Maud now plunging wildly and evidently suffering real torture from the subtle titillation she was being made to undergo. Then after a short pause and a significant glance at each other they applied their feathers to Maud's cunt!

"Ha! ... ha! ... don't!—in mercy's sake stop!" Maud almost shrieked, writhing frantically and straining at her fastenings. Half alarmed at the effect of their action Helen and Alice stopped and looked at me as if for instructions. I glanced at the clock, there was rather more than one minute left —I felt positive that Maud could endure the sweet agony for that time and that it would make the ensuing fuck all the more delicious to her—so I determined that she should go on being tortured, so I signalled to them to re-commence—and to prevent the house from being alarmed I held my handkerchief firmly over Maud's mouth so as to stifle her cries. Promptly Helen and Alice complied, their eyes gleaming with lustful enjoyment at the sight of Maud's naked body quivering in agony; applying their feathers again to her cunt they tickled her delicately but cunningly all along its sensitive lips and when these poutingly opened involuntarily under the stress of the titillation and disclosed the coral flesh of her interior, Alice delightedly plunged her feather into the tempting gap while Helen amused herself by tickling Maud's clitoris, now distinctly visible in angry excitement! Maud by now was nearly frantic,—twisting, wriggling, squirming and screwing herself madly in vain attempts to escape from the torturing feathers— and in spite of my handerchief the shrieks and cries were distinctly audible to us. It was evident that the limit of her powers of endurance was being reached and that she was on the point of hysterics, so I signalled to Helen and Alice to stop; just as I did so she cried frenziedly "Fuck me, Jack! Oh fuck me!" In a moment I was on her, with two strokes I buried my prick in her raging volcano of a cunt and began to fuck her. Hardly had I started than she spent deliriously! I suspended my movements for a few moments during which I kissed her ardently—then with renewed lust and unsatisfied desire I again began to fuck her, the sensation of holding her naked struggling but helpless body in my arms and the knowledge that she was tied down and at my mercy imparting a most extraordinary piquancy to the operation! Furiously I rammed into her, deliriously she responded to my fierce downthrusts by jerking herself madly upwards! Then the heavenly climax overtook us simultaneously—and just as she for the second time spent rapturously I shot my boiling tribute frantically into her, she receiving it with the most exquisite quiverings and thrills

As soon as Helen saw that the ecstatic crisis had come and gone, she and Alice unstrapped Maud; and as soon as I slipped off her they carried her off, while I retired to my room for the necessary ablutions. But to my surprise Helen came in before I had commenced. "Alice is looking after Maud, so I have come to attend to you, dear!' she said archly, and sweetly she sponged and freshened my exhausted prick, finally kissing it lovingly.

I asked her if she thought that Alice would be equal to twenty minutes torturing such as we had administered to Maud, also whether Alice's cunt was fit to receive me again. To the latter enquiry she gave a decided affirmative and added that Alice was eagerly looking forward to be fucked, and she agreed with me that we had better reduce the term of Alice's torture to fifteen minutes. I asked with a smile if either she or Maud proposed to fuck Alice, so that I might arrange accordingly—she replied that she would not as she must reserve herself for her approaching turn, but she would not be surprised if Maud was tempted, only Maud was very exhausted by her struggles while being tickled, and, she added with a conscious smile and blush, "I am almost sure she intends to have me when my turn comes!" So we settled that Alice should be thoroughly well felt by her and Maud, then I was to suck her, then we should tickle her cunt, and finally I should fuck her.

When we returned to Helen's room we found Maud busy attaching the straps to Alice's slender wrists and ankles, and soon she and Helen had Alice securely fastened to the four bedposts. I noted with amusement that they pulled Alice's legs much wider apart than I would have done, in fact so widely did they separate them that lips of her cunt were slightly open. She looked perfectly delicious in her helpless nudity, her pretty cunt being exhibited to perfection—and as Helen and Maud gazed silently at her I could see that their erotic desires were being rekindled. Suddenly they threw themselves on Alice and showered kisses on her— then they proceeded to feel her all over, their hands visiting caressingly her most private parts, after which they squeezed her dainty breasts and kissed her cunt, laughing delightedly as she wriggled and flinched under their provocative touchings.

"Come Mummie, let us see the result of Jack's work last night!" cried Maud merrily—and with gentle fingers they opened Alice's cunt and eagerly inspected its interior, noting with amusing animation the changes caused by her violation. Presently Helen gently inserted her finger into the newly opened passage watching Alice carefully as she did so, laughing when in spite of herself Alice winced when the sore spot was touched; but she confirmed her opinion that Alice was fit to be fucked, thereby receiving from Alice a smile of satisfaction. Then they glanced at me as if awaiting instructions.

"Now Alice, you're going to be sucked!" I said with a meaning smile, to which she responded, evidently not objecting to this sweet form of torture. Turning to Helen and Maud I directed them to play with and suck Alice's breasts while I attended to her cunt; and with charming eagerness they addressed themselves to the exquisite morsels of Alice's flesh and blood alloted to them, preluding their operations with ardent and salacious kisses and then proceeding to feel and stroke Alice's dainty bubbies, now holding them up by their little pink nipples, then imprisoning them between both hands and gently squeezing them,—Alice betraying her rising excitement by her quick flushes and nervous laughs.

Presently Maud pressed between her hands the breast she was torturing so sweetly so as to make the delicate nipple stand up—and then she lovingly took it between her lips. "Oh Maud!' ejaculated Alice squirming voluptuously. Helen promptly followed suit, her action eliciting another irrepressible cry from Alice, now rosy red at the sight of her breasts in the mouths of Helen and Maud and the caressingly tickling sensations imparted to her by the play of their warm tongues on her sensitive nipples. I considered it was about time I joined in the play, so lowering my head I placed my lips on Alice's cunt and fondly imprinted lascivious kisses all along her tender slit. "Ah Jack!" she cried, as she instantly commenced to wriggle divinely; and when I ran the tip of my tongue gently along her cunt's lips and delicately licked and tickled them, she began to agitate herself voluptuously, twisting herself as much as her fastenings would permit and wildly thrusting her cunt upwards to meet my tongue. Presently I noticed that its lips began to open involuntarily; as they did so I forced my tongue between them, thrusting, darting and stabbing downwards as deeply as I could into the almost virginal interior and creating in her almost ungovernable erotic fury, under the influence of which she writhed and tossed herself about in the most lascivious fashion. It was clear that she was quickly approaching the blissful crisis—so withdrawing my tongue from her sweet orifice I seized her clitoris between my lips and sucked it fiercely while my tongue cunningly tickled it. This finished Alice off—with an indescribable wriggle she spent in delirious bliss and collapsed in rapturous delight, punctuating the spasms of her ecstasy with the most voluptuous quivers and thrills, then lay inert and exhausted, with turned up and half-closed eyes. But very soon she opened them again, and murmured faintly "Oh, please kiss me!" Instantly Helen and Maud threw themselves on her and showered loving kisses on her helpless cheeks till they restored her to life again; then they tenderly sponged and washed her cunt and gently got her ready for her next torture, while I removed from my lips and moustache the traces and remains of her spend.

When I returned I found Alice was herself again and keenly curious to know what now was going to be done to her. In response to the enquiry in her eyes I leant down and told her we now proposed to tickle her cunt—did she think she could stand it? She trembled nervously then said "I'll try—only stop me from screaming!" "Then we'll gag you, dear!" I said, and carefully I twisted a large hand-kerchief over her mouth. "Now, darling,"—and I signalled to Helen and Maud to commence to torture Alice.

It was just as well that I gagged her, for at the first touch of the feathers on her sensitive cunt the muscles of her arms and legs violently contracted as she involuntarily tried to escape from or at all events to dodge the tickling tips—then when this natural movement was frustrated by the straps she shrieked in spite of herself as the feathers continued to play on and between the lips of her cunt then struggled and wriggled frantically! A delighted smile now appeared on the faces of Helen and Maud at the sight of the delightful agony that Alice was suffering and joyously they continued their delicious occupation of tickling her cunt! Alice now was an exquisite spectacle—in her desperate efforts she twisted and contorted her lovely naked body into the most enticing attitudes, while the sound of her stifled hysterical screams was like music to us! And although it was only a few minutes since I had fucked Maud, my prick became rampant and stiff, as if eager to renew acquaintance with Alice's cunt. It was evident that the subtle titillation was trying Alice severly, but so delightful was the sight of her struggles and wriggles that I allowed Helen and Maud to continue the sweet torture, till Alice hysterically begged me to stop it—which I then reluctantly did.

As I removed the gag from her mouth she gasped "Oh Jack! It was awful!" "But you liked it dear!" I said with a smile. "Well, yes!" she admitted with a constrained laugh, "but it is too exciting for me! —please don't torture me any more!" she begged prettily. "Very well, dear!" I replied, "But then you must end my torture!" and I pointed to my rampant prick. Alice blushed, smiled, and then nodded lovingly to me—and promptly I slipped between her legs and bringing my prick to bear on her excited cunt I gently forced it in—using every precaution not to hurt her—till it was completely buried in her warm, throbbing and fleshy sheath.

"Ah!" she murmured rapturously as she felt herself possessed again by me but this time without pain! I clasped her closely to me till her breasts were flattened against my chest—and then I set to work to make Alice taste the pleasure of being fucked!

She was terribly excited both by the tickling her cunt had received and by her eagerness to again experience the exquisite raptures she had enjoyed in my arms the previous night in spite of the pain of her violation; and as I commenced to move myself on her slowly but sweetly I could feel how she was straining at her fastenings in order to accommodate herself to the sensations of the moment—then as I proceeded to fuck her she murmured ecstatically "Oh! ... oh! ... my darling! ... how . . heaven ... ly!," as she closed her eyes in rapture and wriggled and quivered under me voluptuously as she felt my prick working up and down in her cunt. Soon the blissful ecstasy began to overwhelm us both—Alice agitated herself under me in a perfectly wonderful way as I rammed furiously into her; then her body suddenly stiffened, an indescribable thrill quivered through her as she rapturously spent—at the same moment I shot into her frantically my boiling tribute of love —and then we both collapsed in delicious transports, oblivious of everything but our voluptuous sensations!—Alice enraptured by the exquisite pleasure that she was now fully able to taste, and I

overjoyed at again having fucked her deliciously
dainty self.

We soon came to ourselves. Meanwhile Helen
and Maud had set Alice at liberty; and so after a
long passionate kiss I slipped out of her and retired
to my room accompanied by Maud, Helen taking
charge of Alice. Sweetly Maud attended to me,—
then somewhat eagerly she asked what I proposed
to do to her Mother, confessing with a blush that
she was longing to enjoy her!

"Certainly do, dear!" I replied, delighted at the
prospect of again seeing the Mother and daughter
relieving their lust by means of each other, naked.
Joyfully Maud kissed me, and we hurried back as
Helen an Alice had returned and were awaiting
us.

Alice evidently was full of elation at her newly
acquired sexual freedom; and eager to enjoy her
privileges she caught hold of Helen and drew her to
the bed, at the same time calling to Maud to help
her to fasten Helen down to the four corner posts.
With great glee Maud complied, and very soon
Helen lay extended on her back with her limbs
strapped to the four posts and a hard pillow under
her bottom, absolutely at our mercy.

"Now Maud, you may have your Mother to
yourself for the next five minutes," I said; a vivid
blush surged over Helen as she heard her fate and
glanced half shamefacedly at her daughter, who
however smiled lasciviously at her with the assured

128

air of a conqueror. Alice ranged herself alongside of me, slipped her arm round me and with her unoccupied hands gently played with my balls.

Maud bent down and kissed her mother first on her lips and then salaciously on each breast and finally on her cunt; then seating herself alongside Helen she gently ran her delicate forefinger along the lips of her mother's cunt.

"Oh Maud, don't!" cried Helen, shifting herself uneasily and squirming deliciously under the licentiously free touches of her daughter's finger—but Maud continued deliberately to irritate her mother's cunt till she had worked Helen into an almost uncontrollable degree of erotic excitement, making her plunge and wriggle and twist herself in the most voluptuous manner. It was a charming sight to watch the daughter's delicately slender forefinger at work on her mother's sexual organ half hidden in the luxuriant growth of hairs that crowned Helen's cunt, driving her slowly to the very verge of spending but forbidding her the blessed relief, and making her tug wildly at her fastenings in her semidelirium—till no longer able to endure the maddening desire to spend Helen cried agonisedly, "Oh Maud, to finish me!"

With a gratified smile Maud leisurely mounted on the bed and placed herself between Helen's widely parted legs, and with eyes glistening with lust she arranged herself on her mother so that their breasts and cunts rested on each other—then fiercely seizing Helen's helpless body she set to work to rub her cunt against her mother's. "Ah! darling!" exclaimed Helen in ecstatic delight, as with half-closed eyes she surrendered herself to be fucked by her daughter, jogging herself spasmodically upwards so as to press her cunt more closely against Maud's. Soon their movements became furiously tempestuous, especially Maud's who plunged and rammed and curvetted herself on her mother s fastened down body in her efforts to bring on the madly desired crisis. Suddenly she cried, "I'm coming!"—and with a hurricane of downthrustings she spent deliciously on her mother's cunt just as Helen with an irrepressible ejaculation of "Ah! ... Ah!" yielded to nature and collapsed, spending ecstatically in her daughter's arms.

As soon as her paroxysms of pleasure had died away Maud kissed her mother lovingly, rose off her and rushed to the bathroom, shielding with her hands her cunt from our inquisitive eyes; but Helen, being tied down, had to remain as she was with her cunt fully exposed, all glistening and sticky from her daughter's spending. With charming confusion and shamefaced blushes she endured our amused scrutiny—then catching Alice's eyes she murmured, "Please, dear!" whereupon Alice prettily proceeded to remove all traces of the double spend; and by the time Maud returned Helen was ready to be submitted to Alice's caprices.

"What now, Jack?" she asked hesitatingly. I

pointed to Alice. "You've got to satisfy her lust now, dear—go ahead, Alice!—" and installing myself comfortably in an arm-chair I drew Maud on my knees so that together we might watch Helen under Alice's hands.

For a moment Alice stood undecided, her eyes wandering over Helen's helpless and naked self; but she set to work to play with Helen's beautiful breasts, which she stroked and squeezed and caressed, finally sucking each in turn, keeping her eyes fixed on Helen's tell-tale face as if to access the result of her toying. What she concluded evidently encouraged her, for with a wicked smile she armed herself with a finely pointed feather and placed herself by Helen s side in a position from which she could command Helen's cunt.

"No, no, Alice! Don't tickle me!" cried Helen hastily as she nervously tugged at her fastenings, laughing nevertheless at her predicament. Alice however only smiled mockingly at her and proceeded to apply the feather to Helen's cunt, passing the tip lightly but searchingly along its sensitive lips that were still excited from the friction induced by Maud's cunt. "Don't, Alice!" again cried Helen, squirming charmingly—but seeing that she was doomed to undergo the sweetly subtle torture she nerved herself to endure it, clenching her teeth and firmly closing her lips so as not to cry out.

Then followed a lovely spectacle! Having had her

131

own cunt severly tickled, Alice had learnt where the most sensitive and susceptible spots were and also the most telling way in which to apply the feather to them. Availing herself of this knowledge she so skillfully tickled Helen's cunt that in a very short space of time she had Helen struggling and writhing in the most frantic contortions, straining at her fastenings so frenziedly that the bedposts began to creak—her closed eyes and clenched lips and her heaving breasts and palpitating bosom heightening the provocative effect of her naked tossing and agitated self. But although she heroically refrained from screaming it was evident that she was fast reaching the limits of her powers of endurance; and the gaping of her cunt dumbly indicated the excitement erotically raging there. I succeeded in catching Alice's eye and signalled to her to stop, which she instantly did—and not unwillingly, for her flushed face and glittering eyes betrayed the lustful concupiscence that now possessed her and which she was longing to satisfy by means of Helen's naked helpless body. She dropped the feather and impulsively threw herself on Helen, and was proceeding to work herself on her as she had seen Maud do, when Helen gasped brokenly "Wait ... a moment ... darling! ... " Although she now was absolutely trembling with unsatisfied lust Alice sweetly and sympathisingly suspended her movements; she clasped Helen tightly to her, her breasts resting on Helen's and showered ardent and salacious kisses on Helen's flushed cheeks and quivering lips till Helen had sufficiently collected her disordered faculties—when she opened her eyes and smiling amorously at Alice and murmured "Now, darling!"

Alice needed no encouraging! Gripping Helen tightly she furiously rubbed her cunt against hers, her deliciously youthful figure and her frenzied and uncontrollable but exquisitely graceful movements forming a wonderful contrast to Helen's matured but voluptuous body so rigidly and relentlessly strapped down into practical passivity. So new was Alice to the art of fucking that in place of prolonging the exquisite pleasure and slowly bringing on the sweet climax she concentrated all her energies to procuring the satisfaction of her erotic lust. Wildly she rubbed her cunt against Helen's till the ecstatic crisis overwhelmed them both—then simultaneously they spent, Alice with a rapturous cry of "Auntie! ... oh! Auntie! ..." accompanied by the most voluptuous thrills of carnal delight while Helen ejaculated deliriously "Oh! ... oh! ... Alice! ... dar ... ling!! ..." as she lasciviously quivered in her amorous transports!

In silence and spell-bound, Maud and I had watched Helen and Alice, but the sight was too much for Maud; and when Alice set to work to fuck Helen, Maud whispered hoarsely to me "Jack! ... Jack! ..." and agitated herself on my knees in such a way that her desire was unmistakeable

133

Instantly my hand sought her cunt—there was no time for any sweet preliminaries, my finger went straight to her throbbing clitoris and so adroitly did I frig her that just as Helen and Alice were surrendering themselves to their lust and began to spend, Maud also distilled her sweet love-juice with an ecstatic discharge all over my hand!

I let the three women rest undisturbed till the throes of their spending had ceased; then when Alice slipped off Helen after passionately kissing her, Maud seized her and dragged her to me, exclaiming "Show us your cunt, dear!" Bashfully, Alice stood still as we delightedly inspected her sexual organ, all smeared with the love-juice that had proceeded from herself as well as from Helen. I showed her my hand—"This is Maud's!" I said with a wicked smile, wiping it gently on her hairs I added "Now your cunt carries the sweet essence of all three of you, darling!"—to her blushing confusion, which Maud terminated by dragging her off to the bathroom. Helen was still in her semi-swoon looking most fetching in her exhausted nudity; quietly I armed myself with sponge and towel and gently set to work to clean her cunt. This roused her from her torpor—she slowly opened her eyes, but when she recognized me and what I was doing to her she started into full life and hotly blushing exclaimed, "Jack! ... oh darling, that is not for you to do!" Suspending my work for the moment I replied smiling significantly "My darling Helen, as

I am about to be the next occupant of this sweet abode of love, may I not put it in order for my self?"

She smiled tenderly at me and raised her face as if inviting a kiss; and as I bent downwards she whispered softly "Darling, may I suggest my next torturing?" I nodded with an encouraging smile. Helen blushed deeply, then murmured bashfully "Do you mind ... sucking me? I have never had it done to me yet, and I would like to try it! ' "Certainly, dar!" I replied, delighted at her request, then added, "and after that?" She blushed again then replied softly "Fuck me, darling!" Enraptured, I kissed her passionately in token of compliance; then I set to work again, and thoroughly sponged and purified her sweet cunt inside as well as outside—and by the time Maud and Alice reappeared Helen was herself again and eagerly anticipating the new experience she was about to taste.

When the two girls returned I placed them on the other side of Helen—they guessed from my position what I was going to do to her and with expectant smiles they quickly took their places. Then lowering my head I brought my lips to bear on Helen's eager cunt and kissed it sweetly, first in the very centre of her clitoris—each kiss making her shiver with pleasure. Next I began to pass my tongue backwards and forwards along her slit, licking it delicately but provokingly. "Oh Jack! ... oh! ... oh!" Helen exclaimed agitating her bottom and

135

hips voluptuously while a smile of beatitude crept over her face! Seeing that she was now revelling in the erotic sensations aroused by my tongue I continued to lick and tongue-tickle her till her cunt became to gape and pout amorously, when I darted my tongue into her orifice as deeply as I could and tickled the deliciously warm soft interior. This set Helen raging with erotic lust "Oh! ... oh! ... Jack! ... my ... dar . ling! ..." she gasped brokenly as she violently wriggled in lascivious transports as I first tickled this sensitive part of herself with my tongue and then took it gently but firmly between my lips while I passionately sucked it! This finished Helen! Her struggling body suddenly stiffened, a violent convulsion swept through her, and with an incoherent half-strangled cry she spent rapturously with the most lascivious quivers and thrills!

As I reluctantly raised my head from Helen's cunt the two girls noiselessly clapped their hands gleefully, evidently delighted by what they had witnessed; and as Helen was still absorbed in her ecstatic oblivion they accompanied me to my room watching with more amusement the removal from my lips and moustache of the traces of Helen's spend "What next, Jack?" they eagerly asked. "The usual finale, dears" I replied smiling—"only I am going to pull the straps so tight that Helen won't be able to move at all, and also will lie like a log while she is being fucked! When I give you the signal just tighten the straps as much as ever you can, even if she cries out!

Helen had come to herself when we rejoined her, and welcomed us with her usual kind smile; the girls at once kissed her warmly, and eagerly enquired how she liked being sucked. Helen blushingly confessed that she had found it just heavenly! "As good as ... what you are about to receive, Mother dear?" asked Maud teasingly. Helen laughed. "Do not forget, dear, that I have tried it only once, while the other—well, I know and love!" she replied evasively. "Well Helen," I intervened, "I was going to fuck you—would you prefer to be sucked again?" She blushed, hesitated, then said gently "The old way, Jack, please; I like to be in your arms, dear, and to feel myself possessed by you, and to ... spend in response to you!" "Then fucked you shall be, darling!" I replied as I kissed her tenderly—"Shall I do it now?" "Give me a minute or two, please Jack!" she pleaded, then turning to the girls she said softly "Dears, will you try to work me up." "I know a better way for both of us," I said—and straddling across Helen I seated myself on her chest, placed my prick between her breasts, and with my hands I pressed the latter together round and over it, at the same time lasciviously squeezing them as I gently logged my prick backwards and forwards between them, revelling in the delicious contact of Helen's full and soft breasts against my now excited organ—its stiffness together with the provoking friction seeming to communicate to Helen some of its ardour, for in spite of her shame-faced confusion at the sight of her breasts being put to such a use her bosom soon began to heave and palpitate and her colour to come and go. I nodded to the excited girls, and they immediately set to work to pull the straps as tight as ever they could, laughing merrily at Helen's dismay and protests when she found herself practically unable to move at all! "Now, darling!" I said—and working myself backwards over her stomach I slipped into position between her legs, threw myself on her helpless and rigidly extended body, and with one powerful stroke I drove my prick up to its roots in Helen's longing cunt! As I took her in my arms and began slowly to fuck her.

"Ah! .. .Jack!" she breathed blissfully. My sensations were extraordinarily piquant! Although Helen lay motionless under me I could feel that she was involuntarily struggling desperately against her fastenings by her muscular contractions and broken breathing and the agitated movements of her only free part, her head, which she rolled and tossed so restlessly and unceasingly that I had the greatest difficulty in catching her lips to kiss them —while her up-turned eyes, clenched teeth, and half-closed lips indicated that her inability to indulge herself in the relief afforded by even slight wriggles was concentrating the whole of her erotic lust and lascivious cravings in the battle field itself, her terribly excited cunt! The tension was evidently getting too much for Helen, so I set to work to fuck her hard, plunging and ramming myself into her quicker and quicker and more and more wildly till the blissful climax arrived—then madly I deluged the recesses of her thirsting cunt with a torrent of boiling lobe-juice which Helen received with incoherent ejaculations of rapture as she herself spent ecstatically in transports of lascivious delight!

Leaving Helen to lie in happy oblivion I slipped off her, and with the aid of the girls I freed her from her fastenings. Just as this was achieved she came to, and dreamily rolled off her bed; Maud at once took charge of her while Alice accompanied me into my room and again sweetly bathed and dried my exhausted prick—then suddenly stooped down and kissed it lovingly, blushing hotly as she did so. It was the first time she had let herself go, and I augured so favorably of her action that I ventured to whisper as I kissed her "Before long, dear, you must let me teach you how to suck it as well as kiss it!"—in response to which she looked lovingly at me and nodded her head with a tender smile of promise!

We re-entered Helen's room simultaneously with herself and Maud. Helen threw herself into my arms and kissed me lovingly, seemingly overjoyed by her experiences. We chatted together for a little, and then after affectionate goodnights we all sought our respective rooms well pleased with ourselves and each other.

CHAPTER EIGHT

After breakfast next morning Maud started on her visit, Alice and I accompanying her to the station to see her off,—and as it was a fine morning we decided to walk back. While en route a Telegraph lad on his bicycle overtook us, and recognizing Alice he pulled up and handed her a telegram addressed to me; it was from my Solicitors, and it asked me if I could attend at their office at noon on the next day but one to meet the vendors of a property I was desirous of buying. I showed it to Alice and explained that I practically had no option but to attend, and I wired back agreeing to do so; she was very downcast at so unexpectedly sudden a termination to my visit, but when I told her that I could return within three or four days if Helen could again receive me, she cheered up.

But on reaching home we were startled to find Helen in her boudoir wrapped up in a shawl and sitting by a low wood fire. She told us that when she was dressing that morning she was afraid she had caught a cold,—"I certainly have been exposing myself to the air a good deal since you came down Jack!" she said laughingly—and since morning it had become worse, and she was trying to stop it.

I told her that I had been recalled to Town and must go up on the following morning, but that I could be back within three or four days if I might then resume my visit. "Of course, Jack dear!" she replied warmly, "surely you know that we will be only too delighted to put you up again and as often as you like!"

"May I take it that I shall be put up both in the house and in my hostesses?" I asked audaciously. "You may, Jack!" Helen replied with emphasis, as she and Alice broke into merry laughter at my casuistry,—then more quietly she added, "I mustn't put you up myself to-night, darling, for with this cold on me it would be very inadvisable, but I do not know why Alice should not be your hostess tonight, for she has now qualified herself!" and she smiled affectionately and meaningly at Alice, who with sparkling eyes threw herself on Helen and kissed her gratefully exclaiming "Oh Auntie, it is sweet of you!—You don't know how I've been longing to have Jack all to myself for a

142

whole night!' And so it was settled that I should pass the night alone with Alice in her room.

In spite of her protests, Alice and I kept Helen company all the afternoon and evening, during which I managed to find an opportunity of asking Alice to put on her daintiest underwear when she dressed for dinner and also to let me undress her when bed time came,—to both of which requests she gave a blushing promise.

In due course bed time came,—Helen kissed us both lovingly and then said somewhat pointedly to Alice, "A sweet time to you, my darling, please be very careful and run no risks!" With a conscious blush Alice faithfully promised; then we retired to our respective rooms, and when half past ten chimed I slipped noiselessly into Alice's bedroom attired only in my dressing gown, and was rapturously welcomed by her. True to her promise she had not begun to undress; and when I took her in my arms in all her pretty finery, the thought that I was about to take off her dainty garments one by one till she stood naked before me made me thrill with lascivious emotion.

As may be well supposed I had never been in Alice's bedroom, nor had I ever caught a glimpse of its interior. It was a veritable little nest, furnished simply but in exquisite taste, and curiously in keeping with its sweet occupant. On the walls hung some beautiful water colour paintings, and scattered all over the mantel, dressing table, the top of the chest of drawers etc., were her girlish treasures, nick-nacks, framed photos and the hundred and one trifles girls love to accumulate. But in my present frame of mind two articles attracted me— first, Alice's bed, a pretty single bedstead of white enamelled wood covered with a dark bed-spread,— then next, an unusually large cheval-glass that stood across a corner; on the first Alice would lie quivering in my arms as I fucked her, while the second would reflect our naked figures as our hands wandered audaciously over each other.

She seated me in a low easy chair, placed herself on my knees, then threw her arms round my neck and kissed me passionately, murmuring "Oh my darling! it is nice to have you here all to myself, and to feel we can do just whatever we like!" "And what are you going to like, dear?" I asked as I returned her kiss. "Something naughty, darling?" she replied, blushing prettily, "I feel ... wicked tonight!" she added laughing gaily. Clearly my presence in her room and the prospect of having her clothes taken off her by me had inflamed Alice's imagination; and promptly I resolved that I would take the opportunity to initiate her into some of the finer mysteries of the art of fucking!

"We won't waste any time, darling!" I said softly, "I'm not going to leave you until you have drawn out of me every drop of my love-juice, —so you'll have every opportunity of being ... naughty!" Alice hugged me to her in huge delight

144

at this announcement, and kissed me passionately; then obedient to my unspoken suggestion she rose, and with an indescribably subtle gesture she intimated that she stood at my disposal!

I also rose, and throwing off my dressing gown I exhibited myself to her stark naked save for my shoes and stockings. She blushed prettily at the sight, her eyes dwelling fondly on my prick which was beginning to show signs of interesting itself in the proceedings. I slipped my arm round her waist and drew her to the cheval-glass saying, "Let us see how we look!" "Oh Jack!," Alice exclaimed, half shocked at the contrast of my naked self with her fully dressed self so faithfully reflected in the glass—then laughed merrily as she watched my hand wander amorously over her bosom and also her hand as it gently took hold of my prick and caressed it!

"Now, darling, let me undress you!" I said tenderly to her,—" you'll have to show me how to get your dress off you, but the rest I can manage myself!" Alice laughed somewhat constrainedly, then under her whispered directions I removed all her jewellery and ornaments, unfastened and took off her dress, unbuttoned and slipped off her petticoat,—she yielding herself to me but blushing furiously as her attire became scantier and scantier, till she stood in her corset, under which the fringe of her chemise hung provokingly nearly down to her knees and revealed her pretty and slender calves cased in black silk stockings and dainty shoes! I feasted my eyes on her charming dishabille, making her turn herself so that I could view her sideways as well as before and behind, she colouring delightfully at witnessing my admiration —then I resumed my delightful occupation by unlacing and removing her corset after first inspecting her sweet little breasts as they nestled in its pouches. Then I made her draw her arms through the shoulder staps of her chemise and let it fall to her feet; I dealt with her practically transparent vest in the same way,—and then Alice stood before me naked to her waist and wearing only the daintiest of deliciously frilly drawers, black silk stockings and shoes!

"Now see how you look, dear!" I said, and led her again to the glass. "Oh Jack!" she cried, laughing shame-facedly, "I'm positively indecent!" and her blushes redoubled. "I'm going to make you look more indecent still, darling!" I said with a meaning smile, "Please get out that large black hat with the dark feather and put it on." "Oh Jack! what an idea!" she exclaimed in fits of laughter, but nevertheless sweetly complying she put on the hat! "Now darling, stand again in front of the glass and watch yourself as I take down your drawers, and step out of them!" Now red as a rose and trembling with erotic excitement, Alice placed herself in front of the mirror—I knelt behind her, undid the tape fastening of her drawers but kept them in position with my hand—then watching her intently in the mirror I suddenly pulled them down to her feet. "Oh Jack!" she cried as her eyes caught sight of herself naked to the knees, and involuntarily she shielded her cunt with both hands! "Raise your feet one at a time, darling!" I whispered; obediently she did so. I threw her drawers on to a chair, rose, and standing behind her and looking over her shoulder I grasped her slender wrists and drew her hands apart and backwards, revealing the sweet triangular patch of hairs that my soul so loved. "There darling," I whispered, "now you do look both indecent and naughty!"

Alice blushed beautifully as she surveyed her naked self in the glass, smiling at her bizarre nudity with something suspiciously akin to admiration of herself, "Isn't a pity that you can't fuck yourself, darling!" I asked with a teasing smile. Alice turned to me with eyes bubbling over with merriment at my suggestion, and nodded vigorously her assent, then broke into hearty laughter at the idea.

"Well darling, that's impossible—but come to bed and I'll teach you how to fuck yourself on me!" and I led her gently away and stripped her absolutely naked by removing her hat, stockings and shoes. Then I placed myself on my back on her bed, with her pillows beneath my bottom.

Alice looked at me with undisguised astonishment. "Come darling, straddle across me and put me into yourself!" I said invitingly. At once she comprehended the arrangement, and with pretty blushes she followed my whispered directions; and while I supported her with my arms she with her dainty hands lovingly seized my prick and inserted it into her cunt—and when she had sank down on it until it was buried inside her I lowered her gently till she lay on me and cardled in my encircling arms, when I whispered directions; and while I supported her with my arms she with her dainty hands lovingly seized my prick and inserted it into her cunt—and when she had sank down on it until I was buried inside her I lowered her gently till she lay on me and cradled in my encircling arms, when I whispered amorously "Now my darling, the game is in your own hands! I shall simply lie still and leave you to fuck yourself slow or fast as your fancy may dictate!" and kissed her lovingly.

Alice's eyes sparkled with delightful anticipation as I explained her duties to her. She passed her arms round my neck as if to anchor herself on me, kissed my lips ardently as she murmured "Oh darling, it is just heavenly!"—then looking me straight in the eyes and smiling lasciviously she commenced very gently to agitate herself on my prick, pressing her Mount of Venus so strongly down against my groin that our hairs intermingled! She continued this delicious agitation for a little, then her eyes began to flicker and her breathing to be broken—while her bosom heaved and palpitated excitedly against my chest. Soon her movements became more tempestuous—her bottom began to waggle and jog itself up and down more and more fiercely as her sexual concupiscence grew hotter and hotter. She now was in the throes of lust. She pressed her cheek against mine, clutched me more closely round my neck and worked herself furiously up and down on my prick—then spent deliciously with voluptuous thrills and quivers!

True to my undertaking I lay like a log under Alice, holding her plunging body firmly and closely against mine and encouraging her with salacious kisses—but when she collapsed after spending and lay limp and inert of me, I slipped my hands on to her glorious bottom and set to work to stimulate her to fresh exertions by caressing and fondling her rich and plump flesh. Presently with a sigh of deep content Alice raised her head from off my shoulder, and with humid eyes she looked tenderly at me as she imprinted a long sweet kiss on my lips. "Go on again, dear!" I whispered stimulatingly. Instantly Alice's eyes brightened and her limpness disappeared. "Oh Jack, may I?" she exclaimed excitedly. I nodded encouragingly. "Oh darling!" she ejaculated rapturously as she kissed me passionately —then tightening her grip round my neck she re-commenced to work herself voluptuously up and down on my prick!

This time I left Alice to maintain her balance and position on me without the help of my encircling arms; and while she fucked herself blissfully I gently encouraged her by stroking and tickling her breasts as they rested sweetly on my chest, squeezing them amorously when I noticed that the estastic climax was overtaking Alice. Soon she again spent rapturously, kissing me passionately as the spasms of pleasure thrilled through her—then with hardly a pause she set to work to fuck herself more furiously than ever, plunging and raging riotously on me with wild frenzied down thrustings of her tossing and agitated bottom. My powers of self control succumbed under her fierce assault; deserting her breasts I threw my arms round her, gripped her tightly to me, jerked myself madly upwards— then shot my hot discharge into Alice just as she for the third time spent in delicious transports, flooding my happy prick with her sweet essence of love!

As soon as the spasms of pleasure ceased to thrill through her Alice slipped off my prick, and whispering, "Lie still, darling, till I return!" she disappeared, remindful of Helen's parting admonitions. Meanwhile I lay peacefully on Alice's dainty bed, thrilling at the recollection of the exquisite pleasure I had just been privileged to taste with her in my arms, and endeavouring to decide what next I should do to her: but before I could come to any decision Alice returned armed with basin, sponge and towel, and deliciously bathed and refreshed my now flaccid prick—then lay herself down by my side, encircled by my arm.

"Well, dear?" I said interrogatively as I smiled lovingly at her. Alice blushed prettily. "Darling, it was just heavenly!" she replied softly, then whispered, "Jack, I went off three times!" I laughed, then replied, "I know you were very ... naughty by the way you were wriggling on me, dear—any naughtiness left?" Alice nodded roguishly, then broke into merry laughter. "And what particular naughtiness are you now yearning after, dear?" Alice hesitated for a moment, then whispered bashfully, "Darling, may I watch your ... thing grow from what it now is the the big stiff thing it is when you ... put it into me?" "Certainly you may, dear!" I replied smiling approvingly, "and if you like to use your hands and lips you can greatly expedite the resurrection!" Alice raised herself on her elbow and looking radiantly at me exclaimed, "Darling, I'd love to do so!—and at the same time have a real good look at your ... thing for we've been too ... busy up to now!"—and she laughed wickedly. "You're evidently going to be very naughty again, dear, but I suppose I must put up with it! Now let me arrange ourselves for your special benefit!" And shifting my position I placed myself so as to lie on my back across Alice's bed, then carefully guiding her I made her straddle across me and lie face downwards on my stomach, reversed in "soixante-neuf" style, so that her cunt hung just above my face while she had right before her eyes my penis and balls, and free hands with which to manipulate them!

"There, darling! I think that is about right," I said, for while you are satisfying your natural curiosity and ... amusing yourself, you are giving me something to look at and perhaps to kiss if you sufficiently excite me."

"Oh Jack! you are clever—this is just lovely," Alice exclaimed delightedly as she voluptuously wriggled herself on my stomach till she had settled herself comfortably on me—then I felt her soft but intensely exciting fingers gently seize my penis and balls!

As I thrilled with pleasure at the contact of Alice's hands with my genital organs, I accidentally turned my head in the direction of her tiolet table, and to my great delight I saw ourselves reflected in the glass, visible to me but not to her. Meanwhile Alice, thinking herself unobserved, threw off all constraint and set to work openly to indulge her curiosity. I could see the sparkle in her eyes as with rapt excitement she examined my penis and balls, handling them with wonderful gentleness as she pulled my hairs and drew back the loose skin off the rubicond head and caressed my balls, and generally investigated thoroughly every feature of my sexual equipment.

Presently I felt a premonitory shiver run through her, and I could see by the reflection of her tell-tale face in the glass that some fancy or caprice was tempting her, but that she had not yet surrendered herself to it! Alice was evidently hotly debating something in her mind—whether to do it or not —for her colour came and went and her bosom rose and fell in pretty agitation as she played with my private parts!

Intuitively I guessed that the idea of sucking me had suddenly suggested itself to her—and with the object of seeing whether it was so as well as to encourage her into doing it I softly kissed her cunt, then watched her intently in the glass. She shivered violently, blushed hotly, raised my penis towards her lips—then as she lowered her face to meet it she checked herself as if in doubt. Again I kissed her cunt—again another quiver followed by a strangely yearning look at my penis, which now began to swell and assert itself as it rested between her gentle fingers. I tried the effect of a third kiss, and to my huge delight I saw Alice lower her lips to my penis, and felt her lovingly kiss its sensitive head—then after regarding it fondly she kissed it over and over again! With each kiss my penis grew stiffer and thicker and angrier-looking, till it stood erect and rampant; Alice had not only witnessed its resurrection but had brought about the miracle, and a smile of gratified triumph played on her face as she regarded her handiwork!

Now she had to be induced to suck me! Following the same tactics of suggestion I began to lick and tickle her cunt with my tongue. Alice quivered voluptuously and half-closed her eyes for a moment in bliss—then to my surprise she kissed my balls ardently as they lay in the palm of her hand; and after a little hesitation she commenced to apply her tongue to them, the exquisite sensation together with the provocative sight sending me wild with delight! She now was fairly wriggling on me with lust—I thrust my tongue into her cunt as deeply as I could with a darting stabbing action. Alice now raised her mouth from my balls, her face aflame, her eyes simply blazing with lust; then slowly she guided my prick into her mouth and began to suck it ardently while her tongue played lasciviously on and round its now excited head!

My sensations were just heavenly, and the sweet knowledge that I was engaged in taking the maidenhead of Alice's mouth only heightened my ecstasy. My hands had been playing alternately with her delicious bottom and her breasts—but now I flung them round her dainty waist; and clasping her firmly so as to control her plunging wriggles I set to work to suck her into spending. Every now and again I caught a glimpse of her face as reflected in the glass. Alice seemed as if she was in a delirium—her eyes were almost closed, her right hand held my balls and her left hand clasped my penis—she had nearly half of my prick in her mouth, and instinctively she was working her lips up and down on it as if to pump up my love-juice, driving me mad with pleasure. Just then she must be on the verge of spending, so I fiercely attacked her clitoris, and seizing it with my lips I tickled it with my tongue. A violent convulsion swept through her, then Alice spent rapturously, suspending her suction of my prick while the spasms of pleasure thrilled through her, but retaining it in her mouth. I felt myself going! "Stop darling! ... I'm coming!" ... I cried as I struggled to drag my prick out of her mouth—but Alice kept it imprisoned and tightly held between her lips and teeth, then resumed her suction in so delicious a manner as to break down all my powers of control; and no longer able to restrain myself I jerked myself upwards violently and spent frantically in Alice's mouth, shooting my hot essence down her throat, jet after jet in my ecstatic bliss; but as I did so, in spite of my delirious rapture I turned to see how Alice bore the sudden flooding of her mouth with my love juice. To my surprise and intense relief she absorbed my deluge without flinching, swallowing each jet as it shot into her mouth and keeping her lips tightly closed round my prick till the last drop had oozed out and it had begun to shrink—when she drew it out of her mouth, and with an amused expression she watched it shrivel up and dwindle away to a third of its size. Then without a word she rose off me and disappeared, leaving me in a state of confusion and apprehension that can easily be imagined. But whether I had offended her or not, I had to purify myself; and having done so I awaited events.

In a few minutes Alice returned rosy red but smiling happily. I took her in my arms murmuring "Oh darling!" She kisses me warmly and whispered, "Did I do it all right, Jack?" Relieved beyond measure I kissed her passionately, then whispered back "Darling, you sucked me like an angel!" which set her off into silent but merry laughter; and then we lay down together again, Alice this time placing herself on me with her cunt resting on my prick and her arms round my neck.

"Why did you call out to me to stop, Jack?" she asked presently, with a half-smile on her lips, "didn't you want to . . . finish?"

"I didn't know whether you would be willing to let me . . . finish in your mouth, darling," I replied, "and so I tried to make you stop before it was too late, but you wouldn't, and I had to let myself go. Were you expecting it?"

"Yes," she whispered with a blush and a smile— then continued, "you may remember that just before you . . . violated me" (here she tenderly kissed me) "Maud sucked you till you got stiff! Well, when I was helping her to pack yesterday I asked her about it and she told me how to do it and that you would . . . finish in my mouth and that I was to swallow what came from you! So I was looking out for it—but I didn't expect such a lot," she adding roguishly, "it was hard work to get it all down."

I kissed her lovingly. "And you didn't mind, dear?"

"Not after the first swallow," Alice replied laughing and blushing prettily.

"And you'll do it again?" I asked with a tentative smile.

"Whenever you like as as often as you like, darling," Alice replied tenderly as she sweetly kissed me. I gratefully hugged her, and we lay silent for a moment, our lips pressed against each other.

"And what else did you learn from Maud, dear?" I asked with some interest.

"Oh, lots of things, Jack," Alice replied, laughing merrily. "We talked a lot and she told me a lot! Jack, when she comes back, we are going to have a night together in her room, and she is going to teach me some ... tricks," and again she laughed merrily.

"I wish I could be there to see you!" I murmured regretfully, "you two will make a perfectly lovely pair—and to watch you experimenting on each other stark naked would be a treat for a King! You and Maud haven't yet fucked each other, have you?"

"No, not yet," replied Alice, colouring slightly, "no one has fucked me except you, darling, but I fucked Auntie last night!" she added with evident satisfaction.

"And you no doubt will be doing so again before long!" I added with a meaning smile, whereupon Alice kissed, "but don't practice too much with her, dear, for Maud will have been chaste for a fortnight and will take a lot of satisfying, and to have your charming self at her disposal will excite her more than ever. Mind you write and tell me all that you do with her and also with your Aunt," I added, and with pretty blushes Alice nodded a promise.

Meanwhile her sweet hand had not been idle but had business itself by playing with my prick and endeavouring to restore it to life, and it now was beginning to show signs of returning animation. "Jack, you're coming again," Alice whispered delightedly as she redoubled her delicate attentions, "And how will you take it this time, dear?" I whispered. She hesitated for a moment, then whispered back. "Under you darling, just like the very first time!" and slipping out of my arms she bent herself forward, lowered her head, and took my prick into her sweet mouth, and began to tongue it divinely while she stroked and caressed my balls with her gentle little fingers. Promptly my prick responded to her invitation and became stiff and rampant—but so delicious was the sensation communicated by her soft lips, warm tongue that I let her continue to suck me till fear of a catastrophe impelled me to stop her.

Almost regretfully Alice released my prick from its sweet imprisonment in her mouth, and after a final kiss of its now excited and throbbing head she resumed her original attitude at my side and whispered, "Darling, was that all right?" "Simply heavenly, dear!" I replied as I kissed her gratefully, "now turn over on your back and receive the reward of your sweet kindness!"

With sparkling eyes Alice quickly complied, then separated her legs widely, exhibiting her exquisite cunt in the most inviting way. Without delay I slipped on to her, and taking her luscious body in my arms I slowly and voluptuously pushed my prick into her longing cunt, till it was completely buried in her and our hairs intermingled, Alice quivering with rapture as she felt her cunt being thus deliciously invaded. "Twist your legs round me, dear," I whispered. Instantly comprehending Alice threw her legs across my loins and gripped me tightly to her as if trying to force my prick still deeper into her, at the same time hugging me closer against her breasts with her arms.

Our mouths sought each other, and as our lips met in passionate kisses I began slowly to fuck Alice. The moment she felt my prick moving in her cunt she gripped me more tightly than ever with her legs and then commenced to wriggle under me in the divinest fashion, arousing in me the most

voluptuous sensations of lust sweetly being satisfied. Never in all my life had I been in such
close contact with a girl as I then was with Alice. I
was absolutely locked up between her arms and
legs and rightly pressed against her soft warm
luscious flesh, while with fierce desire I clutched
her to me till her delicious breasts were flattened
against me and I could feel every pulsation of her
quivering self as Love's sweet frenzy by degrees
overwhelmed us both, till no longer able to restrain
myself I spent deliriously into Alice just as she for
the second time flooded my excited prick with her
warm love-juice. But our lust was not yet satisfied,
we were made to enjoy each other again, and my
prick remained stiff and rampant in Alice's cunt.
So, after a brief pause during which our lips were
sweetly engaged with each other, we re-commenced
our now lascivious pastime. This time our pleasure
was deliciously prolonged as our carnal rage had
been gratified, and we could devote ourselves to
voluptuous copulation as connoisseurs and revel in
the exquiste raptures attending the satisfaction of
our lust as little by little we approached the heavenly climax. How many times Alice spent I cannot
even guess—she seemed to pass from one blissful
ecstacy to another, her half closed eyes and slightly
parted lips, her incoherent ejaculations and voluptuously involuntary movements as she wriggled
beneath me testifying to the rapturous transports
she was tasting as I slowly fucked her. But before

long it became evident that Alice was getting ex-huasted, and by now I also was furious to "dissolve myself in ecstacies" in her delicious interior. So I whispered to her, "Now, darling, let us finish to-gether." She opened her eyes langourously with a smile of ineffable pleasure, kissed me lovingly, then set to work to second my now vigorous rammings and thrustings. Soon we were fucking each other madly with the most unbridled lascivious fury. Suddenly Alice gasped, "Now, darling . . . now!" at the same time wriggling hysterically under me. Promptly I let myself go, and just as I felt her warm essence bedew the head of my prick again, I spent convulsively into her with a rapture I have seldom tasted, shooting into her every drop of love-juice that I could discharge.

Under the excess of our rapturous pleasure we both lost consciousness. I, at all events, was in a state of oblivion till the chiming of a clock aroused me. It was 2 a.m. I still lay on Alice locked up between her arms and legs, my prick was still lodged up her cunt, and she was still clasped close-ly to me and apparently sleeping happily. I was loath to disturb but it was imperative that we should separate and retire quietly for the rest of the night. So reluctantly I roused Alice with loving kisses; she opened her eyes in bewilderment, and when the position of affairs dawned on her she flushed rosy red, then whispered shame-facedly and hurriedly, "Oh do let me get up, darling," at the same time hastily releasing me from my sweet imprisonment between her arms and legs. Gently I slipped out of her embrace and set her free in turn —then hurriedly we assumed our night gear; and after a tender "Good night" accompanied by many kisses I noiselessly slipped out of Alice's room and regained my chamber.

Next morning I was delighted to see Helen appear at breakfast, and apparently all right again, though a little pulled down. She had been into Alice's room, and in the absence of the latter she gently chided me for allowing Alice to indulge her newly acquired sexual privileges to a possibly injurious txtent. Just then however Alice appeared, radiant, a vision of happy satisfied girlishness which effectively dispelled Helen's anxieties; and she then proceeded to chaff us both in her usual kindly way—till Alice seized her and with eager insistence made Helen promise with pretty blushes that on the first night of my return she would place herself at my disposal for the whole night.

In due course the hour of my departure arrived, and after a tender farewell and many kisses I tore myself away from the hospitable mansion where I had passed as delicious a week end as ever had been vouchsafed to mortal man!

THE END

BOOK II

Herewith a novelette which has been handed down by private collectors for a number of years. We feel it covers most comprehensively, the subject of discipline and corporal punishment as it is generally practiced in the home.

OLD FASHIONED DISCIPLINE

It has been said that truth is stranger than fiction. Perhaps that depends on what one considers strange.

In our town, just big enough to have a high school, are two families with a good deal in common. My family and the Turners, both comfortably well off, are both headed by a widow, 35 and 40 years of age respectively. They have between them five children of school age. Mrs. Martin, my aunt, adopted me five years ago. I am now 17 and her daughter Cora is 19.

The Turner family consists of Mrs. Turner, tall, beautiful, and stern, and George, 16, Vera, 17, and Doris, 18. We are all students at high school and Cora will graduate this year.

About four years ago Auntie and Mrs. Turner, firm friends for many years, apparently came to the conclusion that their families were slipping out of control, and they decided to do something about it. Well, they settled on a course of action that for them has been a complete success; for us kids, however, their scheme has been painful and humiliating. They must have thought out everything with great care. They made rules of conduct and set out penalties for their breach to include us all. As a safeguard against possible resistance, the two of them tackled us separately and privately, and within a few days they brought us all safely under the rule of the rod.

There were great outcries of indignation, but I don't think any culprit has ever made any real resistance. I cannot say we are unhappy under the new order, painful as it is, and our stern parents boast that they have the best behaved family in town. Over this somewhat remarkable background, I draw a veil of anguished tears and go on to tell of an episode that profoundly affected our lives.

Auntie arranged for Janet, the daughter of an

old friend, to stay with us while taking a secretarial course in town. Janet turned out to be a really lovely, well-stacked brunette with a friendly manner. She was most cordial to Auntie, but, being rather self-important, she was sweetly patronizing to the rest of us and none of us liked that a bit. Cora particularly resented it. She frequently made snippy remarks about our "wonderful behavior." Once Auntie drily observed, "They are not always so well behaved, but rigid discipline quickly improves them."

"Yes, of course, that would account for their nice manners. Indeed, you are to be congratulated, Estelle dear," rejoined Janet airily.

"Thank you, my dear," said Auntie gravely. And then, significantly, "You and I must have some private little talks on the subject of discipline." Janet replied that she would be delighted.

We were sure they did have such talks but had no idea how much, if any, of the Turner-Martin code was disclosed to Janet. However, at the end of Janet's third week with us, Auntie, all smiles, told us.

"There's to be a picnic for all of you tomorrow. Unfortunately Janet and I can't be with you for the fun. We are having Mrs. Turner to lunch, but I think Janet won't miss the picnic too much. She will be entertained here."

Cora and I dutifully thanked Auntie. As soon as we were alone, Cora burst out happily, "This is it,

Gerald! I'd love to be at the intimate little lunch tomorrow. I know exactly what Mamma meant when she said that arrogant cat would be well entertained. She meant well chastised!"

"What makes you say that? And even if you're right, do you think that she'd submit? She's even bigger than Doris Turner."

"Silly boy, haven't you noticed how meek she is with Mamma lately? And how quick she agrees with just everything Mamma says? Oh, she'll submit all right when those gracious ladies start on her. You'll see!"

After the picnic, we all drove back to our house. Cora had guessed right about the reason for the lunch.

Our house is quite secluded, in the midst of a two-acre plot. The most secluded place in the house is the recreation room. It is a very large room and it is here that most of the family punishments are given. In one of its many cupboards are hung in neat array straps, paddles, and Auntie's favorite instrument, the famous—or perhaps I should say infamous—Scottish tawse. It is a wicked little affair of thick leather about three inches wide and fifteen long, and has five slits at the business end, forming sort of fingers; fingers that sting abominably.

There is not much furniture in the room, but one item is outstanding—the massive old chaise lounge that sits before the fireplace. Auntie bought it two years ago and had it remodelled. The high, broad head has a curved depression with a restraining strap on either side, admirably suited and very effective in securing in position the waist or neck of anyone leaning over the head or kneeling on the seat. Along the sides hang other straps for a like purpose. Auntie calls it "the chair of Applied Discipline."

We all trooped own to the rec room. The scene that met our gaze brought gasps of astonishment and then some covert tittering from the Turner kids.

Mrs. Turner and Auntie, wearing severe, plain black sleeveless dresses, were seated on the "chair" nonchalantly chatting and enjoying a cup of tea. Standing in the corner, sobbing spasmodically, dejected, her disheveled hair framing a tear-streaked face, was Janet, her head bowed, her hands clasped before her. She was the very picture of a penitent.

"Did you have a nice time, children?" beamed Mrs. Turner. Then, continuing in tones of quiet authority, she pointed to the sobbing girl. "This girl was an honored guest, but I'm afraid she has been badly spoiled and her conduct here was disruptive to family discipline. So much so, that we decided that she must go home. However, she begged to remain and her wish has been granted. Her status is now very different; now she is one of you. She will share the pleasures and responsibilities of our families and, like you, will be subject to our necessary discipline. She is inclined to be haughty, impudent, lazy, untidy and disrespectful to her superiors. Those faults we shall cure. She has had an exemplary whipping on her bare bottom which, I am sure, she will remember for a long time."

There was a buzz of excited chatter at this cool matter-of-fact announcement, and in a few minutes Auntie brusquely ordered Janet to her room. And, believe me, she lost no time in obeying. The Turners left soon after, and the subjugation of Janet passed into history.

For a few days Janet sulked and avoided Cora and me. I expect the poor girl was ashamed, though she need not have been. We are all in the same boat. However, gradually she settled into her new role. She now said "Auntie" instead of the familiar "Estelle," and was very, very carefully polite and submissive to Auntie, as well as most friendly to Cora and me. I accepted her friendliness at once, but Cora remained cool and distant.

"Why can't you be nice to her?" I asked Cora.

"Listen, Gerald," she answered tensely, "you just don't understand girls. That big simpering Janet treated me like dirt under her feet for three long weeks, and I intend to make her pay dearly for it. Oh boy! Will I ever sting her big fat behind for her when the time comes!"

Her vehemence shocked me. "You actually mean to whip her?"

170

"I do and I shall. You will see, my sweet passive little cousin!" she purred.

No more than ten days after Janet's initiation, Cora and I brought home unsatisfactory reports from school. Auntie was very angry about the reports. "You should know what to expect for these!" she snapped, waving the offending reports at us. "Gerald's hardly surprises me, but you Cora! I am very disappointed in you. Go to my room, the pair of you, and take the tawse with you. I'll attend to you shortly. And you, Janet, your room is a disgrace. Tidy it at once!"

On what small things our fate sometimes hangs. Had Janet meekly answered, "Yes, Auntie," and obeyed at once, I suppose that would have ended the matter. Maybe she was tired and irritable. At any rate, I was amazed to hear her say petulantly, "Oh all right Auntie, I'll do it, but not right now, I'm too tired."

For a moment there was dead silence; then, white with anger, Auntie exclaimed, "Mistakes I can overlook, but deliberate disobedience, coupled with insolence, I punish with pleasure! You go with the others, Miss!"

"Oh Auntie! Please! I didn't mean what I said. I'll tidy my room this very instant!" cried Janet, realizing the wrath she had provoked.

"You will go to my room this very instant instead, for a sound whipping on your bare bottom!" Auntie promised.

A strange thrill went through me at her words, and I flashed a picture of lovely, curvaceous Janet, half naked, her bottom dancing and bouncing under the tawse. I'd never had such thoughts about seeing Cora or the Turner girls in that position, perhaps because they were all so much like sisters to me, and I was usually too busy anticipating the feel of the whipping on my own rump to be aroused by what I saw. But Janet, a near stranger whose body I had bared in my mind often, produced a gush of excited blood through my veins as I followed her still clothed swaying buttocks down the hall.

Cora had fetched the tawse, and while we were waiting in Auntie's room Janet bemoaned her careless words. "Oh, what ever possessed me to answer like that? Oh Cora, I'm terrified!" She trembled a bit as she looked for comfort to my gloating cousin.

"I've no sympathy for you. If you are silly enough to practically ask for a tanning, I hope you get it good. Or perhaps you were rude on purpose and really want a spanking—is that how it is?" inquired Cora searchingly.

Janet blushed to the roots of her hair. "Well, not with that awful tawse," she said.

"So our proud, haughty darling welcomes a smacking from those in authority over her, so long as it doesn't sting too much. Is that right?" queried Cora softly.

"Why, I—er I—well, I adore your mother," stammered the blushing, embarrassed girl.

Cora laughed sarcastically. "Oh, don't bother confessing, I can see through you like glass. You really want it, but gently. Well, I'm sure you will get what you want, and much more besides—and that part will be most interesting. Instructive to you and enjoyable to me!"

At that moment, Auntie appeared. To our surprise, she was dressed to go out.

"I find I must go out at once. I may be very late, so your correction will have to wait until tomorrow evening. Reflect about it and your naughtiness until then. That will put you in a proper frame of mind for your punishments."

"Please, Mamma, may I say something?" cooed Cora demurely.

"Well, yes, what is it?" said Auntie impatiently, "I'm in a hurry."

"I was just thinking, Mamma dear, that it might put us in an even better state of mind if you order each of us to give the other two a preparatory spanking now."

Auntie pondered for a moment, then she smiled broadly. "It's a novel idea, Cora, and may be a good one. Very well, you arrange it, and we will see how it turns out. Now I must go. Let them be good spankings, mind. Good night children, and remember tomorrow evening!"

My pulse had quickened frantically as I realized

what had just passed between Cora and my aunt. The only thought in my head was that soon I would have Janet across my lap and actually feel her bottom bounce under my hand. I knew I was growing an erection, but was not the least concerned at the moment. I did manage, though, to conceal the excitement from showing in my voice and face. Cora's vow of vengeance never crossed my mind.

Cora assumed command as soon as Auntie had gone.

"All right, let's go. Gerald, you spank us first."

"Okay Cora, over you go across my knee," I grinned. She promptly put her slender body in the time-honored position. I flipped up her clothes and gingerly spanked the seat of her panties with my open hand. I neither dared nor wanted to spank her hard. I smacked for about a minute, and when I released her she smoothed her dress down and said primly, "You silly boy. Mamma intended you to give a real spanking and you know it."

I paid no attention to her words, but nodded cheerfully to Janet to assume the position Cora had taken. I was trembling inside as she draped herself over my lap and I felt her warm curves on my thighs. I was tempted to pull down her panties and remove her girdle. I burned with desire to uncover her bottom but lacked the nerve, and so the opportunity passed. I gave a few tentative pats to both cheeks and thrilled to their soft firmness.

174

Then I began spanking a bit harder and the resilient flesh shook and wobbled under the impact of the blows. The spanking was probably a bit harder than what I had given Cora, but I knew I couldn't have produced more than a pink glow on the white mounds. As I let her off my lap, Janet smiled and kissed me, saying, "I love you for that cruel whipping, Gerald darling."

Cora was less than pleased, though, and said again, "All right for you, but it's not obeying Mamma. Now, you take over, Janet, and you'd better do as you were told."

"Oh, don't be so stuffy, Cora. What Auntie doesn't know won't hurt her." Janet laughed as she seated herself in Auntie's upright chair and drew me down across her knees. Lowering my pants, she smacked noisily with her hand until it stung her too much, then pushed me off to make room for Cora.

"Now to spank Miss Sobersides," she exclaimed with evident amusement, indicating that Cora should get face down across her lap. She gave the merest make-believe spanking and let Cora go.

Perhaps I should have known better, but I fully expected Cora would carry on the farce we had begun. I had forgotten her vow to make Janet suffer for her earlier treatment, but there was an eager light in her eyes as she took her place on the chair.

"Come, Miss Naughtiness, get properly face

down across my knees," cried Cora as she turned back her skirt and her knees to receive her victim. Janet looked a bit alarmed at the sharp command, hesitated for a moment, then lowered herself until her lovely form was sprawled across the lap of correction. Cora held Janet firmly by the waistband of her skirt. Her eyes flashing, her voice slightly trembling with emotion, she spoke imperiously.

"Now, you arrogant minx, you are just where I've wanted you since we first met. In utter ignominy, dangling helpless across my lap, anxiously awaiting to have your big bottom bared for a good sound whipping. I'm going to whip you with the tawse. You will remember how beautifully it stung you when Mamma used it on you."

Janet couldn't help but realize she was in for a real good spanking, and she began to squirm and plunge desperately in an effort to get free, protesting with indignation as she struggled.

"No! No! Cora! You can't mean that! Don't you dare! If you use that awful tawse on me I'll tell Auntie! I will! I'll tell!"

"Yes, do tell her, by all means. But you will get the tawse on your bare bottom just the same," trilled Cora, as Janet continued to struggle even more furiously. Her feet slipped on the broadloom, her hands could reach nothing to grab for leverage; she was, as Cora informed her in honeyed tones, helpless. But she struggled on and on for fully five minutes before she dropped exhausted, still where she had started, with her rear in one of the very best positions for spanking. I could see that all through her frantic squirming and jerking Cora held her in place with the greatest ease.

The rebellion thus ended with Cora triumphantly saying, "Have you quite finished your silly wriggling? Because I can wait, you know."

"Yes," whispered Janet choking with emotion.

"Splendid! and now, with your ladyship's kind permission, or without it if necessary, we will arrange your skirt and slip suitably," Cora said, with a great deal of sarcasm.

I watched fascinated as Cora deftly dropped her right knee and pulled the front of Janet's skirt forward and again raised the knee under the more than ample posterior. Then she flipped up the back of the dress, revealing the spank spot clad in frilly flared leg panties over her taut girdle. Cora unfastened the garters, then pulled the cute little panties down to Janet's knees. The girl squirmed under this indignity. I gasped at the sight before me—long, well molded legs, topped by her big round behind, tightly encased in its girdle, out of which popped most alluringly three or four inches of plump, pale pink cheeks. I held my breath as Cora made the final act of preparation for a whipping. Amid pathetic little protests, Cora rolled and tugged the girdle well up on the culprit's waist. I sood transfixed for a moment until Cora snapped:

"What are you staring at? Hand me the tawse this instant!" Then taking the tawse—that most dreaded of instruments—from me, she gripped the rolled up girdle firmly and began to whip Janet.

Her technique for imposing the utmost in anguish and humiliation was superb in its simplicity. She waited after each stroke for her victim to regain her composure enough to truly appreciate the next stroke to the fullest measure. Meanwhile, she lectured Janet to shame her still further.

The tawse cracked down with explosive force to the tune of Janet's yelps of pain as her beautiful behind bounced and quivered.

"This is the reward of naughtiness!" Smack! Smack!! "And to respect your superiors!" Smack! Smack!

By now Janet was sobbing wildly, writhing and gasping out little broken pleas to be let off. Her frantic movements were exposing far more than her scarlet bum, and I was torn between sympathy for her plight and the arousal her nakedness caused. Cora gave a mocking laugh at her unahppy pleas and went on with the work she seemed to enjoy with great relish.

"Let you off indeed!" Smack! Smack! "Of course I will, when I have whipped you to my entire staisfaction!" Smack! Smack! "And I'm not easily satisfied!" Smack! Smack! "Your bottom shall be well whipped!" Smack! Smack! "Like this!" Smack! "And this!" Smack! Smack! Smack!!!

Smack!!! "Now, will you promise you will obey?" Smack! Smack!

"Ow!!! Yes! Yes!! Y-e-s-!!" Janet panted frantically between her sobs and squeals.

"Then this will remind you of your promise!" Smack! Smack! Smack smack smack!!!

At this stage, Janet was practically hysterical, so Cora lectured her no more, but continued to whale the red, unprotected seat on the lap of correction with, if anything, increased vigor during the last flurry of smacks.

At long last, she pushed disdainfully the well whipped girl off her lap and ordered her to bed.

In a daze, I watched the subjugated girl leave the room. I say subjugated because no doubt was left that Cora had done just that to her. I was so completely engrossed in the masterful demonstration I had witnessed, as well as the animated display of Janet's intimate parts, that I had forgotten my turn was yet to come. My memory was quickly refreshed.

Cora, dominant and supremely confident, turned to me: "Well, Gerald, are you prepared to receive your spanking?"

I had no illusions now that she intended to let me off with a token spanking as we had done with her. Truly I was in a dilemma. A thousand crazy thoughts chased each other around in my brain. Cora, tawse in hand, seated herself, ready for my chastisement. Could I appeal to her sense of fair play to treat me as I had her? One look at my determined, imperious cousin told me I could not. She wouldn't even listen. Could I make a break for it and stay out till Auntie returned? No, for my thoughtful cousin had sweetly locked the door and also removed the key. Suppose I simply defied her? Well, she had Auntie's orders and far more important, she had that formidable tawse in her hand. And, if I did manage to resist, I'd only get a double dose later from Auntie. She seemed to read my thoughts.

"If you have any foolish idea that you can evade your just punishment, forget it! For you know perfectly well in your heart that you are going to be well spanked, don't you?"

I sat on the bed twisting my hands in dispair. It seemed an eternity when I heard myself answer in a low choking voice, "Yes, I know, bbbut—"

"There's no 'but' about it boy. Stand up! Hand me your belt!"

My mouth was dry as I shamefacedly pulled off my belt and handed it to her.

"Hold out your hands!" she ordered.

"You don't neet to tie me."

"Hold out your hands!!" I obeyed and she strapped my wrists tightly together.

With that act, I passed the rubicon. Resistance was out of the question, and she could now punish me at leisure.

She drew me close to her right side and gripped

either side of my beltless pants, pulling them down slowly and surely until they collapsed in a heap at my ankles. Faintly I hoped that she would leave me my brief shorts, but alas, they followed my pants, thus depriving me of my last shred of dignity. That is if a fellow about to be spanked can be said to have any dignity.

Having cleared the decks for action, she folded back her skirt to avoid crushing it into wrinkles, and incidentally giving me a generous glimpse of gorgeous silk clad legs and creamy thighs, that on another girl at another time would have been most interesting. Just now I was much too preoccupied with other thoughts. And how!

She drew me down and balanced me across her lap, tucking my shirt well up on my shoulders. I quivered as I felt her cool hands slowly gliding, appraising the area she meant to whip. Strangely, it seemed proper and right for my upstart cousin to punish me. All I really thought about at the time was the pain to come.

Without more ado, she picked up the tawse and started to lash my rear in the same methodical way she had tanned Janet's. The stinging was simply awful and it didn't take me long to commence roaring and squealing. Between strokes I found myself almost incoherently promising—to be good, to be obedient, and above all, pleading to be let go. For indeed I'd had enough.

Cora paused, draping the tawse across my hot

stinging seat. "Why Gerald! You are making more fuss than Janet did. Actually, I've barely begun to warm your bottom yet. And I promise you most sincerely I am going to whip you every bit as soundly as I whipped her."

With that, the awful sonorous smacks resumed. How many I got, I've no idea—but it was far worse than any whomping I'd had from Auntie or Mrs. Turner. The next thing I remember, I was on my tummy in bed, sobbing bitterly and stinging like fury.

It must have been hours later that I heard a soft sound at my door. I twisted my head to look just as the door quickly opened and closed. The room was quite dark, but I could dimly make out a form leaning against the closed door. A moment later Janet, wearing a cotton nightgown, was standing over my bed. I made a grab for the covers but she stopped me, saying, "It's all right. I've brought some salve for your bottom. Did she whip you badly too? I could hear you sobbing."

"No worse than you," I said, stunned by the fact that she was standing by my bed and I was naked. The burning in my seat was for the moment forgotten.

"This will be nice and cool on your hot skin. Let me rub it in and take some of the sting out of it." Not waiting for me to answer, she sat on the edge of the bed and opened the jar in her hand. I jumped as I felt her gentle hand touch my soreness, but then the soothing salve was being rubbed tenderly all over my buttocks, and the fire behind was gradually replaced by new fires within. "What awful welts," she murmered sympathetically, as she traced light fingers over the raised skin.

I gave a great sign as she stopped massaging, both for the easing of the sting and the pleasure of her touch. She hesitated for a second, and then said haltingly, "Would you please do the same for me, Gerald dear? I just know it would feel wonderful."

I somehow managed, in my excitement and confusion, to take the jar from her hand. Then I boldly brushed my lips across hers and said, "That was awfully sweet of you, Janet. It feels much better now. Lie down here and let me soothe your poor bottom now."

I made room for her on the bed and knelt beside her as she lay face down. I felt more eager than shy as I liftd her nightgown well above her scarlet rump, and put a gob of salve on my hand. I rubbed as gently as I could until I could feel that some of the heat was leaving her sore flesh. It was as if my hands were moving without any directions from me as they continued to glide over her bottom long after the salve had done its work, and I heard a little contented coo from Janet that told me that for her too, the salve was not the only consolation she received. Without any conscious thought on my part, my hand lingered at the top of her thighs and

I had an almost unbearable compulsion to stroke the softness between them. Janet must have sensed my desire—more likely, shared it—because just then she rolled onto her side, turned her head toward me, and whispered:

"Gerald, we'd be punished terribly for this if Auntie or Cora should find out. But we could make each other feel so good, and after a whipping like that ..." Her voice trailed off for a moment. "Let's just kiss and touch though, dear, and be very quiet."

My blood was pounding furiously and my body felt like one great throb as I lay back on the bed and took the beautiful, once haughty Janet into my arms.

Next morning I was siff and sore. My seat was a mass of ugly dark red welts and, though the sting had gone, it still hurt abominably. I had to force myself to concentrate on the ache in my bum as Janet came down for breakfast in order to hide the flush of pleasure I felt at the thought of what had happened the night before. Janet had left my room only a few hours before. She sat down very, very gently, and I gave a wince of sympathy as her pained bottom made contact with the chair. Cora and Auntie were all smiles.

"Cora has given me a full report of all that happened last night and I'm sure you both richly deserved what you got. Now, off to school with you.

I shall speak to you again after dinner," Auntie declared sternly.

Janet went off to her school and I to mine. I could hardly bear to sit on the hard seats. It was torture; and, in addition, I couldn't work for thinking about what might still be in store for us at home when Auntie meted out her share of our punishment. What conflicting feelings surged through me, between dread of Auntie and eagerness for the meeting Janet and I planned for the next day, which was Saturday.

We ate dinner that evening in silence. My eyes kept wandering, but always ended up on the tawes which ominously lay on the buffet. We were so uncomfortable that I was really relieved when Auntie spoke sharply, saying:

"I was shocked that you two would dare to disobey my orders to spank each other soundly. And did you both disobey? Did you Janet?"

"Oh, I wish I had obeyed. She couldn't have whipped me any harder in any case," said Janet with a wan smile.

"It's too late to think of what you might have done. And you, Gerald, did you disobey too?"

"Yes, Auntie," I sighed.

"Very well, you must both know that I'm very annoyed and most disappointed in you. And I am more then pleased with Cora, who not only obeyed, but proved herself most capable by giving you a thoroughly sound whipping. Indeed her conduct so impressed me that I have talked with Mrs. Turner and we enthusiastically agree that Cora shall be allowed and encouraged to help enforce discipline in our homes. So my children, I hope you will be delighted to know that Cora now has our full approval to punish any of you if you break any of the rules. You should know them quite well, so there should be no difficulty there. I have decided you shall take over between you Cora's share of the household duties, since she is to take over this disagreeable task. Now, as a symbol of her authority, I am presenting her with this good tawse, which she has used so well, and also with this key to the instrument cupboard."

Cora looked most demure but underneath I'll bet my charming cousin was just reveling in her triumphs.

She thanked her mother meekly and said she would try to be worthy of the confidence placed in her. Janet and I looked at each other goggle-eyed. We were utterly bewildered at this new turn of events. Sort of stunned, I asked Auntie, "And will Cora still get punished?"

Auntie smiled sweetly and said, "Yes, Gerald, of course, if she is naughty in the future. But I rather expect a great change for the better in her deportment since by the same agreement, you two shall punish her if she misbehaves. I think she'll want to avoid that. Now for the good news. The chastisement I promised you for this evening is cancelled. I think you have already paid the penalty, and if Cora hasn't paid fully, it is the fault of the two of you."

"Don't you think they should be punished for deliberate disobedience last night?" asked Cora silkily.

"If you think so my dear, but postpone it and consult Mrs. Turner. She may wish to see you demonstrate your prowess."

Janet and I commiserated with each other later about the new situation. Cora had fallen into her position so quickly and we knew she would show no sympathy for us or have any qualms about using her power at every opportunity. We were quite sure there was no way we could avoid frequent punishments in the future.

It was late the next evening when we met in the woods a quarter mile or so behind the house. I was much bolder now, and took her in my arms at once for a long, exciting kiss. As we lay down on the soft grass Janet told me of the summer she had spent at camp the year before. She had learned quite a lot from the boys in the neighboring counselor's camp when she and a girlfriend would sneak down to the lake shore after hours. I was trembling with eagerness as she described in whispers what had taken place. We spent a long hour in the darkness then, as she patiently and thoroughly shared her experiences with me. By the time we made our way back to the house, Cora and the terrible tawse seemed a distant threat.

It was no easy matter, though, to keep and renew our glow of pleasure in the days that followed. Cora gave us imperious orders to do this and do that whenever we were within earshot. I was really kept jumping, what with housework and school work as well as my regular duties.

Cora certainly blossomed. She no longer looked nor acted like a school girl. She wore high heeled shoes and did her hair in a more mature fashion. She was unmistakably the mistress and we the underlings. She gave her orders with supreme confidence, usually ending with a "And do it quickly and properly or I'll smack your bottom."

Happily, we must have pleased her, for she didn't carry out her threats—possibly because she was afraid that if she proved to be too great a tyrant Auntie would remove the favored status from her. At any rate, when most of her threats failed to materialize, our anxiety began to abate. Unquestionably she was enthralled with her new status. She also meant to graduate and so worked hard at her school work. She hoped to graduate with honors and thus cast shame on Janet and me. Meanwhile, we did her chores and met, whenever we could, behind the house for respite from the slavedriver.

Unfortunately, the quiet was the lull before the

storm. One Friday just as dinner was over, she gave commands.

"There is a small matter to be attended to children," (she copied Auntie's form of address in the most humiliating way), "you will recall your disobedience when I last punished you. I shall reward you for that little mistake tonight. Report to me at the rec room at seven thirty sharp. You, Miss, put on your tightest panties, skirt, blouse and slippers—that's all you'll need. And I warn you both—be prompt now. Go and change for you have only ten minutes."

We hurried down, Janet trembling and clutching my hand. "Oh, Gerald, she's really got a rod in pickle for us. She's been saving it up for us, I just know it, and I'm all goose pimples!"

"Me too," I whispered. As we entered the rec room, every light was on. Cora, seated on the chair, was grim and businesslike. The ping pong table was pushed to the wall and Auntie sat primly on one of the chairs in front of it.

"You may sit down, culprits," said Cora sternly.

Hardly had we done so when Mrs. Turner swept in majestically with her tall and willowy doughter Doris in tow. She is a stunning blonde of 18, nicely rounded and curved in all the right places. Instinctively I knew the reason for her presence. Indeed, Cora's authority seemed to be increasing as rapidly as her appetite for domination. Mrs. Turner significantly locked the door and sat beside Auntie, motioning her daughter to sit beside us. Doris seemed a bit bewildered at seeing Cora sitting where only our parents had sat before.

"Cora, as I told you, my daughter has been impudent, lazy, and disobedient during the last week, thus earning for herself a good whipping. And this punishment I wish you to administer here and now."

Full of confidence, Cora stood up and kicked off her high heeled pumps as she replied, "I shall be charmed to oblige and obey you, dear Mrs. Turner." Doris jumped up, her eyes blazing with outraged indignation as she croaked, "Mom! what nonsense is this? That cat Cora won't touch me! You can't really be serious Mom. I will take it from you, but not from a school kid! Let her just try— I'll show her!!" Then, turning to Cora, she stormed, her face red with anger and humiliation, "You go to hell! Don't you dare lay a finger on me or you'll be sorry!"

Undaunted by this outburst, Cora stepped up to her. Without her pumps, Cora is about four inches shorter than the formidable looking opponent Doris. Cora's hand flashed out slapping Doris' face hard, right and left. The fight was on. They grabbed each other's hair and yanked furiously, swaying and circling around the ample space between us and "the chair." They both squealed with pain and rage and soon it began to look as though Cora had met her match. When, suddenly, Cora drew back her right hand, balled her fist and drove it with terrific force into the pit of Doris' tummy. The girl gasped for breath and relaxed her hold on Cora's hair. Following up her advantage like lightning, Cora let her have two more punches, right and left to the stomach. That ended the fight, Doris collapsed to the floor, all doubled up, gasping and moaning. Instantly Cora pounced like a tigress. She flipped Doris on her face, then straddling her bounced with all her might, knocking out any bit of breath left in her body and leaving her like a limp rag.

Cora by now had the situation well in hand; calm and serene she asked Auntie for a restraining strap from the chair. Receiving it, she wrenched the limp girl's arms behind her back and strapped the soft forearms to the elbow at each side so that they were folded above her waist.

By this time Doris had got her wind back and began to struggle, but it was too late. Cora had won and no matter what the culprit did now, she had no chance of escaping her punishment. She should have realized that, but foolishly when Cora got off her, she got up and started to kick out wildly. Several good ones landed on Cora's shins before she got behind the refractory Doris and pushed her by the ears to the high end of the "chair."

In one swift fluid motion, she pushed Doris down into the depression in the "chair" head and cinched the restraining strap in place about Doris' waist. This had the effect of forcing Doris down until she was bent over at an ideal angle and she was, of course, completely immobilized. Auntie and Mrs. Turner were delightd.

"Congratulations, my dear," beamed Auntie.

"And mine too. You managed her splendidly. And don't spare the guilty girl's bottom after the trouble she's been," smiled Mrs. Turner.

"For her silly rebellion, I thought of giving her a dozen strokes with Mamma's nice thin, bendy cane and a good spanking with the tawse as the chastisement she came for," said Cora in a most respectful tone.

"Certainly, my dear. I quite agree with you and I hear you have found the tawse most satisfactory."

"Oh yes, I really have, Mrs. Turner," answered Cora silkily, as she went over to her helpless victim, swishing the cane as she went. Doris' skirt and petticoat went up over her shoulders. Her little panties soon glided to the floor. Her garter belt Cora removed with a flourish. She was devastatingly beautiful to behold. The pale ivory of her glorious hemispheres and long smooth legs all undraped reminded me of a huge peony, her white petticoat the petals, her luscious legs the stem. Her symmetry was almost perfect. It seemed, no matter how naughty she had been, a pity such beauty must be marred by the rod even temporarily. And that soon Cora's competent hands would have her behind a fiery red.

Doris took her caning like a trooper; she gasped with pain as the awful cane came singing down, but she didn't really yelp before the sixth stroke. Then as the next six hissed down relentlessly, she had to kick, dance and squeal, her lovely form bouncing to the time of the rod. Twelve very red, well spaced welts marked her from waist to thighs when Cora laid down the cane. Then she picked up the tawse and, cracking it in the air a couple of times, she stood and began to spank.

"Now, Miss Impudence, you are going to learn it does not pay to disobey your mother. I'm going to apply three dozen good sound smacks to your very spankable bottom and I hope you will enjoy it as much as I shall," said Cora sarcastically to the weeping Doris.

Doris shrieked and sobbed from the very first stroke, writhing, twisting and squirming her bottom under the smarting caresses of the tawse. Now the tempo of her dance was fast and furious, her shrieks filled the room.

At the thirty-sixth stroke, Cora with smug satisfaction written all over her face, laid aside the strap and left the well punished girl palpitating in her humiliating pose, sobbing her heart out, her whole rear a deep crimson crossed with the deeper marks of the cane, and turned her attention to her next victim.

"Janet, you are to be punished for disobedience, are you not?" she inquired sharply.

"I suppose so," answered Janet.

"You suppose so!" snapped Cora. "I told you to prepare and I hope you did so! You suppose!! Take off your skirt!"

With nervous fingers dear Janet fumbled with her zipper and in a moment stood revealed in nothing but a white frilly blouse and a pair of skin tight nylon panties.

"Hand your panties to me, you naughty girl, as an abject token of your submission," Cora ordered.

Quivering noticeably, poor Janet stepped out of her panties and meekly surrendered the little garment symbolic of her ignominy.

"Now lie over the lounge Doris has just vacated. You shall have two dozen excellent stingers with the tawse. Doris will stand close and watch closely to realize the spectacle she was—if she can see through her tears," said Cora scathingly.

While the ladies discussed Cora's performance, Doris sobbed and moaned in anguish as Cora applied the tawse with vigor to Janet. Quickly Janet's shrieks and sobs joined Doris in a duet of misery as Janet's rear squirmed.

I sat watching the humiliating and painful spectacle of Janet's punishment, all my desperately protective urges squashed by Cora's oppressive presence, and waited fearfully and anxiously for the moment I too would be yelling and squirming under that hellish tawse. I grew more apprehensive as each stroke brought my turn nearer.

Having finished with Janet and allowing her to don her panties behind the head of the chair, Cora led me by the ear to an ordinary chair, then hauled me across her knee as though I was a small boy. A shudder of humiliation and a thrill of fear went through me as she yanked down my pajamas. She held me firmly and slipped a new device on her hand—a glove with a palm and fingers of stout leather stitched to it.

"Your disobedience was not as flagrant as Janet's, so I'm going to let you off lightly and just smack your bottom with my nice new leather spanking hand. I hope it will remind you to obey in the future."

My tanning probably only lasted five minutes, but it felt like an eternity. Like the others, I yelled and wriggled. The "hand" stung like fury and of course it was humiliating, but it was just nothing to what she'd given me before with the tawse.

"There now, stand with your back to the ladies and don't dare move!" she snapped.

Loud were the praises heaped on the triumphant Cora. "You are really wonderful, my dear—a disciplinarian par excellence if ever there was one. You will certainly command respect and obedience," gushed Mrs. Turner.

They must have gone on chatting for more than half an hour. Presently Cora, excusing herself, announced, "They are sufficiently composed now. I will have them serve coffee."

"Splendid! and you will join us, of course," exclaimed Auntie, still beaming with approval. I was sent to don a pair of bloomers with an opaque front but a transparent rear. When I returned, the girls were bare from the waist down with a little apron concealing the front of their bodies and leaving them some little modesty. The white aprons accented the red of their bottoms greatly.

In the kitchen the girls, sobbing and burning, prepared the coffee. I didn't know what I was supposed to do, I only knew that I was only too glad to be out of that awful room.

"I'll get Cora for this if it's the last thing I ever do," swore Doris as she gently touched her red behind.

"Oh come, Doris, be sensible. How can we 'get her,' as you put it? She simply conquered us. We had to submit and we will continue to submit. After all, you have to admit that she is really and truly a super whipper," replied Janet.

"I don't care. I hate her and she'll never whip me again," choked Doris.

"Like to bet?" asked Janet archly. "Well let's get in with the coffee—and don't forget, honey, Mistress Cora has that tawse and she may find your bottom irresistible, so for Pete's sake let's not drop anything."

Doris made no misstep and, coffee over safely, Mrs. Turner rose to go home.

"Before you go, Doris, I want to speak to you. You have been punished for disobedience and daring to resist, but I recall you dared to say I could go to hell. That was an unladylike expression and I will not tolerate it, do you understand?" said Cora sternly, the tawse swinging in her hand.

Poor Doris didn't feel defiant now. She took one look at the tawse and mumbled, "Yes."

"Say 'yes, Miss,' " demanded Cora.

"Yes, Miss," Doris repeated sullenly.

"Good. Now for that unladylike language, come here right after school next Wednesday. Be here at 4:30 sharp for a little lesson in manners, my dear child."

By that time, Cora had subdued and whipped both Verna and George. Cora was well entrenched and in full, undisputed authority over us. Auntie and Mrs. Turner seemed happily satisfied to leave most discipline to Cora. She applied it strictly and all work and duties were carried out promptly. What more could they desire? As time passed, Cora revealed more and more her capability for ruling. Every punishment she gave was calculated to impose the utmost in pain and humiliation to the offender of the moment. She made a ceremony of the act of submission and usually insisted that the culprit go through a long and elaborate preparation for chastisement. She added to the stock of punishment accessories. She had invented the spanking glove and now she made a pony pole—a broomstick with three short straps about nine inches apart at one end. This ingenious device fastens on the folded forearms behind the back. Thus secured, the operator grasps the protruding end of the stick and the culprit can be made to control his movement to a small circle around which he or she is urged with the tawse.

"Why do you stay, Janet?" I asked one evening as we lay exhausted on the grass.

"Oh Gerald, I just don't know. It's too complicated for me to give a straight answer. You see I truly do adore Auntie. At first I was shocked and then enthralled when she told me of the spanking arrangements you'd undergone for years. And how the home now ran like clock work and how your behavior had improved. Well, I had never, nver been so much as slapped and living with you I used to wonder and imagine what a spanking was like. There is some subtle magic about it, you know, Gerald," she smiled. "Frankly, I was dying of curiosity, and Auntie sensed it, I'm sure. Well, one day she said, 'You know, Janet, you really are a spoiled girl and glib as you are I really ought to treat you as I do my own children. I think perhaps I'll phone your mother.' Well, that decided me. Blushing, I answered, 'Oh no, Estelle, don't phone mother! If you think perhaps—'

"She said, 'I certainly do, my dear, but I warn you, my hand is heavy and when I spank it hurts.'

"And so I got my first spanking there and then. And I have to confess that although I smarted I loved her for it—and felt strangely excited. She gave me many more spankings right up until that fateful picnic day. True, they were a little harder each time, but still they were mere child's play to what we all endure now. I guess Auntie was just conditioning me for that first real severe whipping she and Mrs. Turner gave me. Oh boy, was I ever surprised!"

"So now the big spanked girl is as resigned to the code as the rest of us?" I grinned.

"I think I am," said Janet pensively. "You know, at secretarial school I've heard it said my manners are charming. And anyway, I'm attracted to the whole business, painful as it is. So there!"

We talked a bit then about Cora. Certainly she is a different proposition from the adults. They simply and only punish to maintain discipline and improve us. But with Cora, her personal triumphs have brought out a natural, arrogant pride. There seems nothing she won't do to increase and exalt her wide authority. One would think she was a despotic queen and we her servants to be whipped at her merest whim.

"You may be attracted, honey. I don't think I am. But we are powerless anyhow," I mused, a little chilled by my thoughts.

"You know, Gerald, I have an idea. At present she has five targets to hit. If she had more, we wouldn't get it so often," said Janet.

"It's an idea, but where do we get more targets?" I asked.

"You may be surprised, but there are others. I've been thinking a lot—" she replied. "There is a wonderful subject in class and I know she's ripe for subjugation. She's a woman, 25. To conquer her would flatter Cora's ego enormously. I know it'll work because Sandra and I exchange some confidences and she has confessed that she would like a taste of the strap."

"A taste," I snorted. "Why, our Cora would flay her alive."

"So what?" shrugged Janet. "I'm really only obliging her anyway. If she gets more than she bargained for that's her lookout. Anyway, I've spoken to Cora and she's really elated at the prospect. I'm to have Sandra here at 7:30 tomorrow. There, now, I've told all. Clever, hm?"

At 7:15 on the eventful eve, I stole down to the rec room and waited in comfort, sitting on a folding chair in a cupboard of mammoth proportions. Soon Cora entered and switched on two spot lights centered on a space around the "chair." Then she sat down to wait.

Cora was dressed in a clinging black satin sheath, low cut and without sleeves, long black gloves and high heeled black shoes, her raven hair confined at the nape of her neck. She was authority personified. Even I was a little awed.

The "chair" was covered with an afghan, thus hiding its awful purpose. Cora was positively majestic to behold. Her whole being exuded relentless dominance. I thrilled and shuddered at the thought of what I was about to watch. At 7:30 on the dot, Janet came in leading Sandra by the hand to the circle of light. She hadn't exaggerated a bit. Sandra was ravishing. A tall blonde—big and exquisitely proportioned. She wore a long, smart coat and a little red hat. Looking rather ill at ease, she stood there gracefully in the spotlights. I am sure she was on the verge of tears—her hands were twisting nervously.

"Stand there darling," said Janet, taking her coat and hat, under which Sandra was clad in a short tight skirt, barely knee length, and a ruffled white blouse—no doubt dressed according to instructions. Janet stood beside the uncomfortable girl and made a low bow.

"This, Miss Cora, is Sandra Watt, the willful young lady I was telling you about."

"I am aware of that," said Cora imperiously. Then with a contemptuous glance she addressed Sandra:

"Well, I'm told you are 25 and so far have never been whipped?"

"Yes, Cora, that is so," she admitted, blushing under Cora's searching gaze.

"You will address me as Miss!" snapped her inquisitor. "Stop fidgeting and stand rigid and at attention when I speak!"

Immediately the girl straightened and put her hands stiffly at her sides.

"Janet tells me you would not find a taste of the strap unwelcome?"

Sandra, blushing furiously now, stammered, "Well—I—er—that is—I didn't exactly say that. I meant—well, something like that might be interesting—but—."

Cora cut her off sharply. "I agree it will be interesting—very! Now understand your position: if you surrender to my authority, and I think you will—won't you?"

Faintly Sandra whispered her reply, "Yes—er—yes Miss."

"You are a sensible girl, but I warn you I shall tolerate no nonsense. I expect and will have instant obedience or you will suffer the penalty. This evening you shall have your taste of punishment and unless I miss my guess, you will need whipping quite frequently in the future. You'll find I have a stong arm and a good variety of instruments to chastise you warmly with."

"Oh—but—please, er, Miss, I think—I hope—I'm sure one experience will be enough," Sandra cried in distressed tones.

"I will be the judge of that. Consider yourself lucky I allowed you to come here. You will do well to forget you were an independent young woman and to remember you are just another naughty girl under my authority about to have your posterior whipped."

Sandra, almost on the point of tears, wailed, "Oh Cora—I mean, Miss Cora—you look so severe. I didn't think—I didn't expect it to be like this—I can't—I don't want to go through with it. Please!"

At this, Cora smiled disarmingly, "Of course I look severe. You should expect that, my dear."

Sandra seemed to have reached an emotional crisis. She smiled back at Cora. "Forgive my foolish protest, I forgot myself for a moment." And so saying, she sank to her knees and kissed Cora's shoes. "I'll submit most humbly," she said fervently.

How very different she was from the fighting Doris. She was even more passively willing than any of us to lick the hand that chastises.

Cora, obviously well pleased, raised Sandra's face between her hands and looked deep into her eyes. "Come, get up—I wish you face down across my lap."

Sandra's big moment had arrived. Meekly she rose and bent over. Her skirt was flipped up, her panties lowered, and her rear was well clapped by Cora's gloved hand. It was humiliating and stinging, but it didn't seem to shame the girl. Frankly, she looked as though she was enjoying it.

Set once again on her feet, she murmured in a dreamy voice, "Thank you, Miss Cora. I thank you from the bottom of my heart for spanking me."

Cora gave a silvery laugh. "You are quite welcome, my girl, but a little premature with your thanks. The ceremony is not over yet. Janet, turn the spots on the chair and turn on the rest of the lights, then strip Miss Impudence to her bra. Let her kneel on the chair and fasten her at the chest and knees—now be smart about it, or I'll warm your bottom for you too!" concluded Cora with a stamp of her foot.

Janet lost no time. In less than two minutes Sandra was in position, her rounded rear sticking out bewitchingly. She looked fearful of what was coming but was docile and allowed Janet to handle her without a protest.

"Oh, my dear Miss Watt, let me congratulate you on having so ample a posterior to offer for correction! It will be amusing to make it bounce!" exclaimed Cora with glee. "Now Janet, lay on the floor before her the cane, the tawse and the martinet. And get me out of this dress—I want freedom of movement," said Cora, extending her hands for Janet to remove her gloves. Then with much solicitation Janet helped her out of her dress. There she stood, completely lovely, in only black satin bra and matching lace trimmed panties, ready to whip.

"Your bottom is perfectly posed. Now I will introduce you to your dancing partners. First you shall have six marks of esteem from this nice swishy cane." The cane hissed down smartly, leaving well spaced welts on the already pinkish buttocks. Sandra gave an agonized yelp as each stroke stung her, but she took it stoicly and neither bawled nor pleaded to be let off.

"Hand me the tawse, Janet," snapped Cora. "This delightful instrument has the loveliest caress and will kiss your bottom just twenty-four times," remarked Cora as she applied the tawse with devastating effect. Sandra's bottom was now writhing wildly, her sobs and squeals almost continuous, and her behind and thighs really crimson. Then Sandra was released from her bonds and ordered to stand in the corner. Meanwhile, Cora refreshed herself with a cup of coffee served by Janet. Presently Sandra had composure enough for Cora's purpose and was called over.

"Strap the pony pole on her, Janet." I'm sure she didn't know what the pole was for, but Sandra meekly folder her arms behind her and allowed Janet to buckle the pole in place.

Cora grasped the end of the pole firmly and could now control her victim, who was able to move freely but only around the pivot of her castigation. Arming herself with a long, fine martinet, Cora began to thrash the plump, outraged target. The awful martinet whistled down again and again relentlessly. Sandra shrieked and danced. She leaned forward, she arched her back, but she was unable to escape a single stroke. Cora's aim was deadly accurate. Sandra seemed to get an idea—she bounded round and round at the end of the stick, urged faster and faster by the stinging blows to her rear. Cora laid on stroke after stroke. I was spellbound gazing at the girl's frantic contortions. Abruptly, Cora threw down the martinet and ordered the culprit released and to kneel at her feet. Somehow Sandra managed to obey, choking on her sobs, tears streaming down her face.

"Your first lesson is over. Remember it well. Now you know what to expect in the future?"

"Yesss, Missss," sobbed Sandra brokenly.

"Very well. Janet will take you home now and I will continue your lessons in obedience very soon."

I was cramped, but I dared not move in my secret place while Janet comforted and petted her well whipped friend. Finally they were ready to leave and Janet, full of sympathy, said, "Oh, darling, I'm sorry. I should never have brought you here."

"Don't have any regrets, Jan dear. I have none. Truly I was scared and I didn't dream she could whip like she does. It was awful, but I guess I'll get used to it like you. All I can say right now is that Cora is the most!"

Janet was quite right. Now that Cora has so ardent an admirer of her technique, she is much easier to get alone with and doesn't spend nearly as much time checking us up and punishing us for the merest trifling error. Cora has taken to spending more and more time devising new instruments. Oh, we still get our fair share, but not nearly so much as before Sandra came along to distract Cora.

Janet and I still meet frequently in discreet places, and I am proud to say that our pleasure skills are improving as well as Cora's punishment techniques. All in all, I can't say I regret the change in household operations that Janet's presence produced, strange though some of them may seem.